THERE'S NEVER BEEN A BETTER TIME TO ~~BUY~~ DIE

a novel

Bernard Meisler

THERE'S NEVER BEEN A BETTER TIME TO ~~BUY~~ DIE

a novel

Bernard Meisler

SENSITIVE SKIN BOOKS

THERE'S NEVER BEEN A BETTER TIME TO DIE
Copyright 2019 Bernard Meisler
All rights reserved.

Cover Photograph: Bernard Meisler
Book Design: Bernard Meisler and Shay Culligan

Published in the United States by **Sensitive Skin Books**.

All characters appearing in this work are fictitious. Any resemblance to real persons, living or dead, is purely coincidental.

No part of this book may be used or reproduced in any manner whatsoever without the prior written permission of both the publisher and the copyright owners.

First Edition 2019 **Sensitive Skin Books**

ISBN: 978-0-9961570-9-4

Library of Congress Control Number: 2019910201

A small section of this book was previously published, in somewhat different form, in The Unbearables anthology FROM SOMEWHERE TO NOWHERE THE END OF THE AMERICA DREAM *for Maggie*

Howard Hawkes: "Who killed the chauffeur?"
Raymond Chandler: "I have no idea."

Chapter 1

Later, as I looked down and watched the body beneath me slowly turn blue, I reflected on the unusual events of the past few days and it occurred to me that mistakes had been made. If I moved fast, I could still forget it ever happened, move on to a higher plane. But first I better tell you my side of the story, so you won't judge me too harshly.

It was about eleven o'clock in the morning, mid-April, with the sun hot shining and a look of no rain for months in the foothills of Mount Tam. I needed a favor from Barney, my business partner—my sideline business, my hustle, that is—so I told him I'd catch him at the worksite. I had a new client in Homestead Valley, an estate sale. Some old lady croaked and now her house was up for grabs. First I stopped at the dead old lady's house, then swung over Barney's. I thought I was doing Barney a favor when I gave him the eight-ball. How was I supposed to know it was poisoned?

That was how it all started and it still seems very strange to me now, almost ten years later. I don't understand it at all. I've thought and thought and I still don't get it. This wasn't murder. I was trying to do somebody a favor and I wind up dead. All right, all right, I didn't get killed—whaddya think this is, *Sunset Boulevard*? I'll admit it, I exaggerate sometimes.

I'm getting ahead of myself. I need to start by telling you about the old lady's house, and what happened up in the attic, or else none of this will make any sense. Not that it makes sense to me, even now. But you'll be more objective about it than me, so maybe you'll understand what happened. Perhaps you can explain it to me when I'm done. So please pay close attention—I might have some questions for you later.

When Charlie got the listing, she called it "Handyman Special w/ Million Dollar Views." We were a small outfit, Charles le Chauve Realty

Corp., based out of a tiny office in downtown Mill Valley. We used to be bigger, but now it was just me and Charlie, my boss. Charlie wasn't French, she was Eastern European I think. I couldn't spell her last name on a bet, lots of XYZs and such. She thought the French moniker made us sound classy and sophisticated.

"Hey Rick," said Charlie, "I got a beaut for ya. A handyman special with million dollar views, over in Homestead Valley."

"Easy access to the 101?" Every house in southern Marin had easy access to the 101, even if it didn't, if you get my drift.

"You got it, kid!"

Charlie was a good old girl, and she genuinely liked me. She even forgave me for my brilliant idea for a high-tech real estate startup, the one that almost brought down the company: a series of interactive CD-ROMs to teach house flipping. We launched in the spring of 2007, and figured we'd start with Ross, the little town with the megabucks. Maybe you don't recall what happened that year—that's the summer the subprime crisis hit, when Jim Cramer delivered his famous "They know nothing!" rant about the Fed. It shouldn't have affected us—and it only affected Marin prices for a month or three before they bounced back—but it was enough to kill our highly leveraged business venture, and almost take down Charles le Chauve in the bargain. You don't remember that? The mini-housing bust before the Big Bust? Me neither, 'cause I was drunk most of the time—how else do you deal with a crisis? Maybe I should have known better. It wasn't all my fault, there was plenty of bad news to go around, but in rapid order Charles le Chauve Realty went from eight folks to just me and Charlie. Charlie forgave me but wouldn't forget. She had me shoveling shit to get out of the doghouse, so she gave me all the dog houses. I was lucky Charlie liked me; anybody else would have fired me for my screw-up.

I rolled up to the old lady's house in my silver BMW 335i, the sports model with the 18" wheels and leather interior. I couldn't really afford it, not after the Ross fiasco, but it was a lease so I didn't have a choice. I was blasting the Dead, the segue from "Seastones" into "Eyes of the World" from 9-11-74. That's a really great jam, there were still some awesome, trippy moments in '74, and Ned Lagin rarely gets his due. You and me both, Ned. Legend had it the band got together before this show and decided they were getting too messed up on blow, so they flushed all their coke and dropped acid instead. If only I'd been that smart.

I stubbed out my joint in the ashtray and checked the curb appeal. A neglected house gets an unhappy look. Or maybe it's the other way around. Either way, this one had it in spades, afflicted with a sort of numbing paralysis, disintegrating in slow motion. What a dump, even worse than the pictures. Ma and Pa Kettle would've turned up their nose at this crap shack. The original redwood siding was cracked, split and peeling, the roof sagged like a swayback horse, and I could hear the single-pane windows ("Original Leaded Glass Windows") rattling. As if that wasn't bad enough, the lot was on a 30 degree or so pitch; at best, the house had foundation issues, at worst it was a mudslide waiting to happen ("In Harmony With Nature"). No sane person would build on a parcel like this. But this is California, so there were plenty of houses just like it on either side, up and down the block, seemingly hanging onto the hill for dear life.

What with all the deferred maintenance, I was thinking we'd put it on the market for 995k. "Great Potential. Bring Your Architect." If we advertised it that way, somebody would snap it up quick, take it down to the studs, spend a couple-three hundred grand and flip it for 1.8 and everybody would be happy. I would have done so myself a year earlier, but I was already stuck in the middle of one of those deals with Barney. Luckily we had a big fish on the hook, with Apple cabbage, because things were starting to slow. Hopefully we could still find a sucker for this dump, somebody besides Lawrence Yun, who believed that housing prices never go down. A quick sale might get me back in Charlie's good graces and I could move on to greener pastures.

I thought the weed would help my hangover, but just taking a gander at this shithole made my headache worse. One of these days I'd remember that just because they called it the 2am Club didn't mean I had to stay there till 2:00 a.m. I opened the glove box, rummaged through the registration and insurance papers and unpaid parking tickets and found a plastic amber prescription bottle. I shook it and heard that soothing baby rattle sound. I opened the bottle. Just three little purple pills left. That was sad. I supposed I could always get more, but these had sentimental value. I dug under the seat and retrieved a plastic pint of Popov. I bit one of the pills in half and washed it down with a swig of the vodka and thanked my Pops once again. I had hoped he'd leave me some dough, or his house, but the bottle of pills I snatched off his nightstand at hospice when he checked out was a better legacy than nothing. I stowed the booze back under the seat and chewed a breath mint. They say vodka doesn't leave a trace, but I'm a belt-and-suspenders kind of guy. Time to go to work.

Chapter 2

I was sporting my business duds: $200 designer jeans, black Tommy Hilfiger polo shirt and black Merrell loafers. I slipped on my summer-weight Zegna wool blazer, automatically placing myself in the top 1% well-dressed of Marin; folks around these parts think nothing of going out for a birthday, anniversary or pre-IPO dinner at the fanciest (read: overpriced) restaurant in the county wearing cargo shorts, Teva sandals and a fleece jacket. I like to dress a cut above the casual multi-millionaires, and it's easy to do so.

I dragged my sorry hungover ass up the mossy stone steps to the old tumble-down house; the yard was overrun with tall grass and blackberry bushes. "Natural Landscaping." Why did some people let their houses get so run down? Takes all kinds, I guess. I rang the bell and somehow could tell even before it didn't ring that it wasn't working. I'm good with stuff like that, intuition, even premonitions. Add the broken bell to the punch list, things to get fixed in the next couple of days before the brokers' open. People were always in a hurry to ditch estate houses, barely waited till the body was room temperature before listing it, too impatient to even spend a week to put in Home Depot laminate flooring, cheap Chinese stainless steel appliances and imitation granite countertops. That shit—we called it Pergraniteel—was catnip for the rubes. But I suppose the dead old lady's kid or grandkid had a tuition payment or needed braces or had a gambling problem or a failing business and needed cash, yesterday. It's none of my business, but if the client wants a quick sale, great, that's how I like it too. Still, even for an obvious teardown like this, I planned on bringing Barney's crew to spruce it up. You'd be surprised how the smell of mold can bring down the price of a house somebody's planning on knocking down anyway.

I rapped softly at the solid wood door, most of the light-blue paint long ago peeled off. I made another mental note to paint it red, make it pop.

An old lady opened up. Not the dead lady—this isn't a ghost story—I don't think so, anyway—although, like I said earlier, I'm still not sure what happened, so maybe it is. It was the dead old lady's sister, the one who'd signed a contract with Charlie last week granting Charles le Chauve a 90-day exclusive right to sell. She'd called me this morning, asking me to please meet her at the house at my earliest convenience, she had something of the utmost importance to discuss. "Great," I said, "sure." What else was I going to say? She wasn't a pain in the ass. Not yet. But she was on her way. I would have ignored her if she'd signed up for a year, but she—or somebody advising her—was savvy enough to insist on the shorter term.

She had paper-thin white skin with deep laugh wrinkles around the eyes. You could tell she'd been hot stuff in her youth, probably around about the same time the Beatles broke up. Or maybe when Elvis got drafted. Despite the early hour, she was dolled up like she was on her way to the Oscars, wearing that famous pink Hillary dress from the first Clinton Administration. It was ten years out of date, and I noticed some loose threads dangling from the shoulder, what we call around in my trade *wabi-sabi*, though we usually apply the term to houses, not clothes, or the people wearing them. "Well hello Mr. Davies, how nice of you to come."

I sensed her sincerity, a rare trait in California. It's nice to be appreciated, made it worth the trouble getting here at 10:00 a.m. on the dot. And by trouble I mean getting out of bed. You'd be amazed how many Californians (including transplants like me) will arrive for a meeting half an hour, or even an hour late, and think nothing of it. Or else just not show up at all and excuse themselves later with the all-purpose excuse, "Dude, I flaked!" and then just beam at you in a very punchable way. A little farther along in the process, once I had her hooked, I could start flaking, send her calls straight to voice mail. At the beginning of a relationship, though, I liked to blow their minds and show up on time.

"It's my pleasure, Mrs. Papadopoulos. And please, call me Rick."

"The pleasure is mine…Rick. And it's Miss Papadopoulos." She smiled wider and—I swear—batted her eyes at me and ushered me in. I followed her into the vestibule. Oh geez, what have I gotten myself into now. Hey, don't get me wrong, I'm not above tapping the occasional lonely client—hell, meeting bored housewives in the middle of the day is one of my favorite perks—but she was a few decades past her sell-by date. But if she wanted a little friendly flirtation, I'm happy to play along. Clients would go away glad, with less profit, if they thought they'd made friends with their realtor. People are funny.

"Can I get you some tea? I just made a fresh pot of Earl Grey."

My ex-wife Gail had turned me on to good tea. Earl Grey, unless it was imported from England—that's the only way to get the best stuff—tastes like sausages to me. "Yes, I'd love some, Earl Grey is my favorite."

"Cream and sugar?"

"Absolutely." She disappeared into the kitchen and returned a few seconds later with an ornate teapot on a silver tray, porcelain cups, a silver milk decanter, the whole nine yards. She'd obviously prepared for my arrival. "Sorry, we're not really well-equipped at this house, I brought the tea service over this morning for our meeting. And I had to feed the cats. We're keeping the kitties here for the time being."

This was not "well-equipped?" What, no frickin' cucumber sandwiches, I thought as she poured the tea. "Are you British, Miss Papadopoulos?" Besides the tea, she was putting on some kind of mid-Atlantic accent. I couldn't help but poke fun at her.

"Who, me? No, native Californian," she said, leading me into the living room.

"Well, what a pleasure to finally meet one! I'm from New York myself, grew up in Rhode Island." The tea was lukewarm and bitter; Trader

Joe's private label, the kind of tea that makes you understand why most Americans don't like tea. It tasted like sausages.

"Rhode Island? You mean Long Island?"

"Close enough." Nobody ever knew where Rhode Island was, not even in New York. For chrissakes, it's one of the fifty states. But I'm used to it so I let it pass. I sipped the nasty-tasting tea while I took in the room. Statues of nudes, fake Impressionist paintings, floor-to-ceiling blood-red velour drapes hanging on iron rods dimmed the light. Very nicely decorated. If it was 1936. And we were in a New Orleans whorehouse.

She sat down on an overstuffed maroon couch, upholstered in a fleur-de-lis pattern. Even from across the room I could see it was covered with cat dander. I'd have to pick up a new lint brush at Bed, Bath and Beyond after this. I always keep a few of their 20% off coupons in my car. You never know when you might need one. "Won't you join me on the divan?"

Divan? Was that a ten-dollar word for "ratty old couch soaked in cat piss"? I joined her on the divan. The springs were shot. "So, what can I do for you today Miss Papadopoulos? I've got a crew lined up, we're going to put on a fresh coat of paint, stage the house with brand-new furniture and I promise you we'll get top dollar for your mother's home."

"Oh my," she tittered, "it's my sister's place. Perhaps I'm not as young as you think I am."

Damn if she didn't bat her eyes again. I felt a chill run up my spine.

"I appreciate all the hard work you're doing, but it's more than money we're concerned with. This house has been in our family for over 50 years. My sister and I grew up here and Sylvia—that's my sister—moved back in here after her...troubles. She had a beautiful place in Ross but she lost it in some boondoggle."

Chapter 3

She paused, waiting for me to ask, but I didn't dig any further—the less I know about my clients' personal lives, the better. I got my own problems. Ross—don't remind me. I knew what was coming next anyway.

"…and we'd love to see it go to the right family, who will make it their own."

And there it is. You hear the good-family routine every time somebody had lived in the house more than ten years or so. People get attached to their dwellings, like hermit crabs.

"Of course, I understand, I'll do my best to find good folks to live in your home." I don't sell "houses"—that's too impersonal. Selling houses sounds like a cold-blooded financial transaction. Me, I sell *homes*—it's not about money or price or value, it's about family, kids, baseball and BBQ in the backyard, the full Norman Rockwell. So of course I wanted "the right family" in this "home"—the right family, of course, being the first people who qualified for a million-dollar mortgage for this shanty. What, does a million clams seem like a lot for a falling-down shack? Hey, this is Mill Valley, one of the most desirable areas in the Bay Area, land is scarce, so you pay for the lot, not the house—excuse me, home. And the lot was big, by local standards, almost a fifth of an acre, even if it looks like a cliffside landscaped by the Addams family. But 40% of its acreage would justify a 4000- or even 5000-square-foot McMansion. Some middle-aged hedge fund manager's recent-college-grad wife would be very happy. And remember, it's not like you're *spending*—it's an investment. Real estate *always* goes up, especially in California, more so in Marin, and even more so in Mill Valley. There's always never been a better time to buy.

"And you say you own the place free and clear?"

"That's right, no mortgage. My sister hated debt, after what her ex… well, never mind, that's old business."

"Great, that makes everything easier." I wasn't kidding. Look up "acceleration clause" in the dictionary and you'd see a picture of this joint.

An orange tabby jumped up on my lap and head-butted me. Cats are like giant roaches with fur. And just like roaches, if you see one, especially in an old lady's house, that's means there's more around, maybe another 100, give or take. I scratched his head. "Ah, what a good kitty!" I said in my best cat-lover's voice. I made direct eye contact with him so he'd leave me alone. I know a little something about cats. He jumped off my lap and scampered off.

"That's Mr. Frank. Isn't he just adorable?"

"That's a fine-looking cat. Very regal."

"He was my sister's favorite." She sighed. "He's mine now."

We quietly sipped our sausage-flavored tea and then Mrs. P put a bony hand over mine. I overcame reflex and didn't pull away. "Mr. Davies, I have a favor to ask."

I swallowed my tea. It didn't go down easy. "Sure, name it."

"My nephew Wilmer usually helps me out with tasks like this. He's… very successful, something with computers, but he's very busy right now."

Wilmer? What the hell kind of name was that? Didn't sound Greek. Or like anything else. But people in California give weird names to their kids. I just read in the *Chronicle* the other day, somebody named their baby Shithead (pronounced "Shith-heed"—or so they thought.) And didn't Angelina Jolie name her kid Shiloh Pitt? I guess if you're rich and famous nobody will tell you.

"I need somebody to go up into the attic and look over some of my sister's personal belongings. I'm sure it's just a bunch of worthless old junk, but I'd feel better if somebody checked it out just to make sure, before we have the open house."

I'd scheduled a brokers' open in a couple of days. That's an open house for other realtors, no public allowed. Gives us a chance to show the house to other pros before it hits the MLS, so they can show it to their serious "clients." That is, the "clients" *think* the broker is working for them, but unless they contracted the broker specifically to be their agent, he's actually working for the seller. Didn't know that, did you? "Happy to lend a hand. I have another appointment in…" I glanced at my Treo. "…48 minutes, but sure." I used to have a Rolex; now my cellphone has to do double duty.

"Oh, I don't want to keep you."

"No problem, it's right over in Tam Valley…"

She raised her eyebrows.

"Don't worry, it's a business call. I don't know anybody who actually *lives* there."

She smiled, relieved, the corners of her mouth turning down, like the smart ladies figured out to do as they got older. Gotta minimize those laugh lines. Or make the work last as long as possible. Yeah, I had her number, a one-time lefty, probably used to get drunk with Pigpen and blow Stokely Carmichael back in the '60s, now she's a limousine liberal on liberal doses of Botox, has a COEXIST bumper sticker on her SUV, and looks down at the folks who live in the neighborhood the wrong side of the hill, where it's always foggy and houses cost 20% less. As if 20% less means they're occupied by bikers and meth labs. Another NIMBY snob. My people.

I put down my teacup and followed her up the stairs. The treads were all out of true and creaked loudly. I put a hand on the rickety bannister but not any weight, for fear of tumbling off the edge. We made it to the second floor landing. No rugs, no furniture, no sign of life up here. Somebody had already cleaned up.

"I haven't been up in the attic yet. I doubt anybody has been since Caleb…passed away."

"Caleb?"

"My sister's ex." She frowned. "It was very unexpected." I couldn't tell if her frown meant she didn't like his unexpected death, or just didn't like Caleb. The French word for brother-in-law is *beau-frère*. It's also the French slang expression for "jerk." Gotta love the French. The language, anyway. I spent a few years in Paris during my wayward youth, so I can *parlez-vous* it a little bit. You know, the basics: *"Où est le métro?"* and *"Je voudrais une baguette, s'il vous plaît,"* and *"T'as pas du shit?"* Fact is, I'm the one who came up with the name for Charlie's company. If we'd had the Urban Dictionary back then and Charlie had looked up what it meant, she'd have—sorry, getting a bit ahead of myself again.

A golf ball hung from a short piece of string attached to one of those pull-down built-in attic ladders. I reached up and had to yank it pretty hard before it budged. It squealed like Ned Beatty in *Deliverance* as it unfolded. I started climbing.

"Watch your step."

I smiled down at her. "I'm up for the challenge." I rose into darkness, reached up till my hand found a support beam. I slid my hand over the rough, unfinished wood, hoping to find a light switch. Something sharp slid into my hand and I screamed.

Chapter 4

I wondered for a second if there was some idiot child hiding in the attic that Mrs. P had forgotten, and he'd stabbed me, protecting his turf. But no, it was just a large splinter.

"Oh my, are you all right?"

"I'm OK," I said, pulling it out. It didn't really hurt, I'd cried out from the unexpected shock, not pain. Between the vodka and the tea, the morphine was dissolving rapidly into my bloodstream. I felt a warm glow on the top of my head. I felt good, like I could do no wrong. "Just a splinter." I groped around some more, gingerly this time. Ah, there it was, a switch. I flicked it and a dim light turned on—the bulb was still good. My lucky day.

"Be careful up there!"

Yeah, no kidding. I crawled through a thick layer of dust on the unfinished plywood floor. Scattered motes swam about me like fireflies. I realized the ceiling was high, so I stood up and reconnoitered. There was nothing to see except one big old piece of furniture, under a white sheet, like in one of those old movies I used to watch Saturday mornings on channel 56. I whipped the sheet off in one quick motion, half expecting Huntz Hall to jump out.

It was a big, solid oak dresser, replete with hand-carved scrolls and filigrees, a big mirror on top held up by an elaborate wooden bow. Had to be over 100 years old. Man, they don't make 'em like this anymore. I held the flashlight up to its surface. The finish was glossy, unscratched, mint condition. Original hardware. Worth five, maybe six grand.

"Find anything?"

"Just an old piece of junky furniture, I think it's some kind of dresser."

"Oh. You better check the drawers, see if there's anything good in there."

"Hey, if I find any spare change, can we split it?"

"Fifty-fifty!" she said, laughing.

I remembered when I was a teenager, the first time my parents left me alone in our house. They went on a trip to the Canary Islands, and I decided, to their chagrin, not to accompany them. I was 16, a pain in the ass and they said OK, fine, be that way, and left me with a fridge full of food, keys to the car and $100. I was a good kid—I did well in school at least, which was their only metric—and I guess they figured why not give me a chance to either be responsible or screw up. Gotta do it sooner or later.

Word got out and my pals came over every day. We'd blast Pink Floyd and the Stones and Bob Marley through Dad's stereo, zonked out on the couch, enveloped in a haze of pot smoke. The day before my parents came home, we were cleaning up the signs of the week's debauchery. "Hey, thanks a lot for helping out guys," I said, "let's do one last fatty to help see us through." Already wasted, I rolled a big joint as *Natty Dread* finished for the 20th time that week. I set the joint down, put Bob back in his sleeve—I always take good care of my vinyl, and hate people who don't treat their records right—put on *Skull and Roses* and came back to the couch and… wha? I couldn't find the joint. What the hell? That was weird, I had it right here. I checked my t-shirt pocket, behind my ear. I looked in the cracks between the couch cushions. Then I pulled the cushions off the couch. Then I looked underneath the couch. Nothing.

Half a dozen frantic high school boys turned the house upside down. Not only did we strip the couch of all its cushions at least three times, as that seemed the most logical spot for the joint to have gone missing, we went to rooms we hadn't entered all week, looked in the basement cedar closet, my parent's bedroom, everywhere. Nothing. Apparently the joint had somehow dropped into the Bermuda Triangle, disappeared without a trace, like it was a liberal Republican.

I was terrified. If my folks found the weed, it was curtains. I'd be grounded, or worse, never left on my own ever again. My parents came home and a day crawled by, I was on tenterhooks, then a week, then three, and then I stopped worrying about it. Wherever that damn doobie had gone, apparently it was gone for good.

Five years later, I was a senior in college, coming home for Thanksgiving; Mom picked me up at the airport. "Something funny happened yesterday."

"Yeah?"

"I had a man over to steam clean the upholstery. I showed him the couch, and he asked, 'Hey, can I keep any change I find under the cushions?' so I said, 'Tell you what, I'll split anything you find in there 50-50.'"

By this time I'm already guffawing, 'cause I see what's coming. "A few minutes later, he comes into the kitchen and says, 'Hey lady, wanna split this with me?' and he's holding a marijuana cigarette."

Yup, you never know what you're gonna find in an old piece of furniture, especially when it hasn't been disturbed in many years. I opened the top drawer. It was packed with once-upon-a-time-top-of-the-line camera equipment: Zeiss lenses, Leicas, even an old Nikkormat. Those babies were built like tanks, and used to cost a fortune. Practically worthless in the digital age, ready for a one-way trip to the island of misfit analog toys.

In the middle drawer were old stereo manuals, Kodachrome slides, and weird souvenirs, miniature stone Mexican pyramids, a blowgun, what appeared to be a fossilized rhino horn. Kinda cool but not exactly in high demand.

The bottom and final drawer was full of old socks and tighty-whitey underwear. OK, now we're getting somewhere. As any burglar worth his salt knows, people stash their valuables—cash, jewelry, stuff like that—with the unmentionables. I dug my hands in, feeling around. Sure enough, one of the pairs of socks felt lumpy. I pulled them apart. Jackpot! A tight roll of hundreds held with a rubber band, maybe ten grand, and half a dozen Krugerrands. Woo-hoo! I slipped the cash and gold into my jacket pocket and kept on poking around, but didn't find anything else. I reached all the way to the back of the drawer. Something was off. Then it hit me—the drawer was too shallow. I pulled it out all the way and peered inside; there was a small wooden box on a little platform in the back. Double jackpot! I reached in and found an ancient cigar box. On top of the box was embossed, "The Turks Head Club, Special, Providence, RI." My old hood. Now what did we have here? Maybe a lost HP Lovecraft manuscript? I opened the lid. Whoa.

Jesus, who did this box belong to, Jerry Garcia? Its contents: a small sheet of perforated cardboard with a couple dozen tiny pictures of Felix the Cat, laughing and holding his belly; a glass vial containing three or four grams of white powder; a bent-back spoon, bottom burnt; three diabetic syringes, still sealed. Wowzers. I slipped the vial and sheet of acid into my pocket. I left the spoon and syringes. I don't use needles—a man has to have a code—and besides, it wasn't my business. Let somebody else discover the family's dirty secret. Then it occurred to me that I better get rid of this stuff before I brought the dresser to my antique dealer. He's an honest guy, relatively speaking, but I'd hate for the authorities to get involved. I carefully placed the spoon and needles in my pocket.

"Well, anything good inside that dresser?"

I turned around and yelled at the portal. "Yes ma'am, some very nice camera equipment and some family heirlooms you might be interested in. I know a guy who'll take the camera stuff off your hands. It's not worth much anymore, y'know what with all the digital and what not, but he'd probably give you a couple hundred for it."

"Found money, I like it! Now come on down before you develop an allergy up there, it's way dusty."

Good idea. I turned off the light and climbed back down the ladder.

"What about the dresser? You said it's in bad shape?"

"Yeah. I'll have my guys haul it out and take it to the dump."

"Oh, that's a tough job. I'll have to reimburse you for that."

I waved her off and smiled. "Don't worry about it, it's my pleasure."

"OK fine, but I insist we share whatever you get for the cameras."

I shook her hand. It felt like holding a wounded bird, like I could crush the life out of her if I squeezed just a little harder. "Deal."

Chapter 5

I handed the camera equipment to the Goodwill guy in the Safeway parking lot at Camino Alto, and he gave me a blank receipt. I wrote in that it was worth $500 as, according to my accountant, that's the most you can claim without raising a red flag. I took the roll of 100s from my jacket pocket and pulled off one for Mrs. P—I'd tell her this was her take from the cameras. I hesitated and thought, why not, she's a nice lady, peeled off a second one, and put the two Benjamins in my wallet to give to her later.

I pushed the start button of my Beemer, the CD player kicked in and Blur came on, nice and loud. It sounded good, felt good, like I was in a car commercial. I headed down Miller and turned into the Taco Bell and ordered a $0.79 burrito at the drive-thru. On my way out, I leaned out the window and tossed the burrito, the burnt spoon and syringes into the trash bin by the exit.

Pulling out onto Miller and heading toward the high school, a guy in a black Lexus SUV came barreling down Gomez Way and cut me off. Why is it always a Lexus? This hood is lousy with luxury cars, Kraut mobiles, giant Hummers, Road Rangers and even the occasional Lambo, Maserati or Ferrari. But when you get cut off—which happens frequently here in the land of entitlement—it's almost always a Lexus. Somebody oughta do a study, get a government grant to drive around southern Marin getting cut off all day long, see what percentages were Lexi. *Lexus*—wasn't that a Henry Miller novel?

I passed the football field, overrun with wild turkeys, on my way to Tam Junction. I turned right on Shoreline, the road lined with enormous overgrown eucalyptus trees. They were beautiful and lent a fragrant scent to the chill morning air. They're also an invasive species, really just a kind of giant weed, and are a horrible fire hazard, a deadly inferno waiting to happen, and should be cut down immediately. But they do smell good. I turned left on Pine and then right on Marin Avenue and pulled up to the construction site where Barney was working, although working is probably too strong a word for what he was doing. The street was steep and I cursed as my Beemer bottomed out with a hideous scraping sound, alerting Barney to my arrival as I came to a stop at the curb.

Barney limped over to greet me. He'd been in a motorcycle accident a few years back, was lucky to have gotten away with just a gimpy leg. He kept on riding his bike. He's kind of an idiot. He's also a weakling—after his wife Cherie ran off with a celebrity chef, he kept paying her alimony, even though the chef was living with her and made five times as much dough as Barney. But he's semi-reliable, which is twice as reliable as most contractors, and does work that stands up to inspection in dim light, so partners we were.

"Hey bro, how you doing?" He rubbed his hands on his filthy jeans before shaking. I waved to the three illegal Guatemalan immigrants who did all the heavy lifting. *"Hola,"* they said and waved back. Nice guys, even if I was pretty sure they were making disparaging remarks about me under their breath in Spanish, calling me a *pendejo* or a *maricón* or whatever. I didn't care, they were good at their job, worked twice as hard as any American, and would do asbestos abatement without permits or hazmat suits, so I let them have their fun.

"Keepin' it real, you?"

"Livin' the dream."

"How's this coming along? Run into any issues?" I was pulling his leg, the good one, though he was oblivious. Barney always ran into issues. He'd been a general contractor since the '80s, but was always taken by surprise to find there were "issues" with 80-year-old do-it-yourself houses. I remembered what this place was like twelve months ago. It was a one-time

San Francisco getaway bungalow, back in the pre-Golden-Gate-Bridge days when the swells took their summer vacations in Marin instead of Maui. Built around 1910. Peeling paint, busted-out windows covered with plastic sheeting, the roof missing half its ancient wooden shingles, yard overgrown. The neighbors were no doubt glad to see the cantankerous old hippie who'd been living there since 1965 take his leave. The hippie, who'd been on SSI for decades, was happy to grab his half a million bucks and piss off to San Miguel de Allende or Vietnam or Portland or wherever it was these days that bums with a little scratch and no desire to work liked to piss off to.

Ask them now, the neighbors probably wished the hippie had never left, even if he scared the kids every day of the year except Halloween, when his was the only non-decorated, non-candy-dispensing house in the neighborhood. A creepy old burnout was better than a half-dozen pieces of earth-moving equipment rumbling around a quarter-acre lot every weekday, all day long, for almost a year now. The bulldozers or steamrollers or whatever that digging thingy is called would lumber back and forth, back and forth, spewing dirty blue smoke into the otherwise crisp, perfumed air, who knew why, back and forth, forward with another great belch of blue smoke, then again backwards, slowly, with the incessant BEEP BEEP BEEP backup warning blaring for 30 seconds. Then, just when you thought it had finally stopped, a minute later there it was again, BEEP BEEP BEEP, on and off, all GODDAMN day long, months at a time, like Chinese water torture. I was glad I didn't live within a five-block radius of this project; everything within it was coated with a fine layer of dust. Amazing the absolute wretchedness people will put up with to live the good life. But too bad for them—this was unincorporated Mill Valley, subject to county regulations, not those of the town, so we could pretty much do whatever we wanted. We had pulled permits—and were doing way more than what they allowed—but prominently posting them on the site kept the neighbors from calling the cops on us and getting us red-flagged.

I watched as the neighbor's gigantic black SUV with a "Keep Tahoe Blue" bumper sticker pulled into their driveway. Mom got out, fit, mid-40s with preternaturally bright blonde hair, her ass spectacular in yoga pants. They don't call this town Milf Valley for nothing. I don't know if the guy who invented yoga pants was a genius, but whoever convinced women it was acceptable to wear them in public, that guy deserves a Nobel Prize. Her kids popped out of the SUV like maggots out of a dead rat's eyes, the girl in a ballerina outfit, the boy in a baseball uniform, still carrying his little bat. It could have been the cover of *White Privilege* magazine. "Zooey! Hunter! Let's go!" Mom said, toting a couple of environmentally friendly canvas bags from Whole Foods. She made an obvious effort not to glance our way.

She hated us because we were part of the gang working on the new house, and we'd destroyed her peace and quiet, and there was nothing she could do about it, as long as we quit at 5:00 p.m. and didn't work weekends. We needed a variance, because the house exceeded 40% of the lot size, and we had to take down some pesky heritage redwoods blocking our new driveway. There was a neighborhood protest at the community board meeting over at the Log Cabin, and everybody had seen the blueprints and artist renderings. They didn't like it, but there was nothing they could do about it; a few palms were greased and we were approved. They had a point—the design *was* over the top, even by local standards. Most of the neighborhood houses were bungalows or cottages, with a few newer McMansions mixed in. But our project was different: 4500 square feet of menacing glass, right angles and steel ("Architectural Gem"). Not what I'd build, if I had my druthers—I thought it looked like a James Bond villain's lair, a car dealership or a giant discount liquor store—but that's what the market demanded. Or it least it was when we'd started the venture—more like a misadventure—a year earlier.

To make matters worse, Barney and friends didn't just knock down the old shack, they chopped down every tree, ripped out every bush and every blade of grass, because they weren't going to be in the right place feng-shui-wise when the new abode was complete. The old driveway, a narrow asphalt path pock-marked with potholes that went straight up the side of the hill, just wouldn't do. Barney had hooked a live one, the client was paying us as we went along, no questions asked, so Barney spent over six months building a brand-new state-of-the-art driveway, constructed to the same code as an interstate highway. Cost: a half million simoleons. The guy we were building this place for had deep pockets, and we were doing our best to empty them.

Barney looked crestfallen, like he always did when you asked him for a progress report. "Dude, you wouldn't believe what we found in there."

Of course I'd believe it, what could it be? Lead pipes for the water supply lines? Asbestos ceiling tiles? Hundred-year-old vintage knob-and-tube wiring? What nightmare hadn't we uncovered on previous renos? I'd read somewhere that some guy in some shithole town somewhere, maybe it was in North Dakota, was fixing up his parents' house and found that the walls were stuffed with old newspapers and comic books for insulation. As he removed the old papers, out popped a copy of *Action #1*, the first appearance of Superman, worth millions. He got in a tussle over it with his sister and they ripped it in half. Easy come, easy go.

"Yeah, I can believe." I knew Barney liked to talk, so I let him. As if it mattered that he found these problems, now that he was in the process of tearing the house down and starting from scratch.

Barney threw up his hands, exasperated. This was his favorite thing, complaining about the shitty job done by a previous contractor, or, even worse, former owners with a handy streak. "We took down a wall in the kitchen, there was unterminated electrical wire behind the old wood panelling! Not even taped, just bare copper! It's a miracle this place never burned to the ground!"

"Heh, too bad for the old owner, he might've collected some insurance jack before he sold out."

"Heh, yeah. Hey, but I got some good news—got a great deal on some Chinese drywall."

"Cool." He didn't have to tell me we were going to charge the client the same as if it were American made, and wasn't full of toxic byproducts. "Listen, I got a quick job for you and the guys. Can you break for a couple of hours? I need you to haul a piece of furniture for me."

"Sure man, no problem. The old lady's house?"

"You got it. Big dresser, in the attic. Bring it by the office, I'll figure out what to do with it later."

"Right on."

"Oh yeah, and here's a bonus for you." I reached into my blazer pocket and tossed Barney the vial of white powder. Barney smiled, winked and slipped it into the watch pocket of his jeans. He knew better than to ask any questions.

"Hey, did you hear what happened?"

I didn't like the sound of that. "No, what?"

"Remember a couple of weeks ago, some chick from the city went hiking by herself, she went missing, they found her body off the Railroad Grade trail a week later?"

"Yeah, she was a Tantric Yoga teacher, right? Didn't they say she tripped and busted her neck on the fall, and tumbled far enough off the path so that nobody could see her? What about it?"

"They just found another one."

"Another one what?"

"Another body."

"Jesus, what the hell?"

"I know, crazy, right?"

"Where? Who?"

"Thirty-eight-year-old girl visiting from out of town, but they said she grew up here. They just found her like ten minutes ago, on the Cowboy Rock trail. You know, the one that goes from Stolte Grove to Four Corners."

"Yeah, sure," I lied. I had no idea where that trail or any other trail was, but didn't want to admit it. People like to hike and commune with nature around here but me, I'm a dedicated indoorsman. Damn, another murder. California is really pretty and has great weather, but it has its downsides—earthquakes, mudslides, brush fires, great white sharks. And, of course, serial killers—the Menendez Brothers, the Night Stalker, the Freeway Killer. And those were just the famous ones I can remember off the top of my head. Oh well, nothing's perfect. "Wait a sec, how'd you find out about it if it just happened? You got a police band radio?"

Barney chuckled. "Check this shit out bro." He handed me a rectangular, black shiny gizmo almost as big as my hand. It was larger than my Treo, and the entire front was made of glass. It was one of those new Apple phones; I'd never seen one in person before.

"Oh, you're a fancy man now, huh?"

"Dude it's freakin' awesome. And I can get up-to-the-minute news on this new Website, called the Twitter."

"What's a Twitter?"

"You'll find out soon enough." He peered intently at his new toy; it was like it held the secrets of the universe. I wanted one immediately, if not sooner.

Chapter 6

I headed back downtown to check in at the office. I passed the high school again and stopped at the traffic light at Camino Alto. School was just getting out and hundreds of kids passed by while I waited for the light to change. If it was still the '70s, I'd say there was some fine-looking tail. But what kind of parent would let their hot 16-year-old daughter leave the house with a pair of super-short, super-tight shorts with the word "JUICY" on the back? Things hadn't changed much since David Crosby wrote that song "Tamalpais High (At About 3)." Made me glad me and Gail never had any kids. I was already up against it. No regrets, or at least no rug rats.

The light turned and I continued down Miller. As usual, traffic backed up in the left lane as people turned, so I moved over to the right lane. I passed Grilly's and the Silver Screen video store. Cars in the left lane were stopped and I kept going through the crosswalk across from Whole Foods and I almost shit a brick as I saw the cars were stopped not to make the left turn but because a young woman was pushing a baby carriage through the crosswalk. I zoomed past her, missing her by a couple of feet but close enough to scare the shit out of me but before I could even recover I heard a siren and saw red and blue flashing lights in my rear view mirror. I pulled over. A motorcycle stopped behind me. A cop got off the bike and sauntered bowlegged toward my car like he was John Wayne.

Before he reached me, I dug around the glove box and found my registration and insurance info; I didn't want my rolling papers, pill bottles or whatever falling out while he was watching. Chance favors the prepared mind. Gurdjieff said that, I think, though I'm not sure who he is. One time I was getting my Mac repaired and the clerk spouted that line at me. It was a good one and now I'm prepared and say it myself whenever I deem it appropriate, as it makes me sound smart. Maybe one of these days I'll read up on this Gurdjieff joker and see what made him tick. I rolled down my window.

"You know why I'm stopping you sir?" The cop raised the jet-black visor of his helmet; he had mirrored shades underneath, straight out of CHiPs. The name tag pinned to his breast pocket read "Justin."

"Yes officer, I didn't see..."

"Listen. This is how we're gonna do this. I'm gonna tell you what you did, and what you were thinking, and you're gonna agree with me, OK?"

I nodded. Why were so many cops such dicks? I was reminded of the time, many years ago, back in NYC, when I was leaving my apartment in the projects on Avenue D and 7th street with two of my friends and we got stopped by a zealous cop. I was the only white man who lived between Houston and 14th. I was about 25, and so was my friend Tim. My friend John was a poet, about 50, and black. John didn't take shit from anybody. He'd done time for selling a kilo of pot back in the '60s. I didn't know it back then, but he'd been one of Malcolm X's bodyguards, was actually standing next to Malcolm when he got shot, and felt guilty ever after about not stopping the bullet. Which might explain his penchant for whiskey and cocaine. Why John and I were friends, what we had in common, despite our age and demographic differences, was literature. And whiskey and cocaine. I was an aspiring novelist myself, which meant I really liked whiskey and cocaine and sleeping till noon, and could justify my sordid lifestyle by scrawling a page or two once a week. We had been doing blow at my place all afternoon and were completely wired. We were taking the elevator down, on our way to drink whiskey at Vazac's, when it stopped on the seventh floor and a young black housing cop got on. Housing cops are real cops. They have low status in the cop world but they carry badges and guns and can arrest you. The cop gave us the once over.

"What's up fellas? Where you coming from?"

"We were at my house," I said.

"Uh-huh," he said. I'm nervous not only because I'm wired to the gills but also 'cause I've got a quarter ounce of cocaine in my pocket. "Where's that?"

"14th floor, apartment C."

"Suuuure. C'mon, let's take a little ride." Despite how scared I was, I had to make an effort not to make eye contact with Tim or John, who were holding in laughter. The eager-beaver cop stopped the elevator and pressed the 14 button and back up we went. We got out and walked across the hall to apartment C. The cop cop-knocked on the door, with the meaty part of the fist instead of the knuckles.

My roommate Tina, the only white girl who lived on Avenue D, answered the door. Tina worked on 3rd and D as a teacher at the day care center. That's how she got the apartment, which was the best deal in Manhattan—$180 a month for a big two-bedroom with spectacular views of the Twin Towers. Everybody in the neighborhood knew who she was—"Hi Miss Tina!" they'd say. Nobody knew who I was and treated me accordingly. Tina was no dummy. She saw us, saw the cop, and played it cool.

"Hey guys, what's up?"

The cop was taken aback; he wasn't expecting a cute young white girl to open the door. "Evening miss. Do you know these gentlemen?"

"Sure."

"What are their names?"

"That's John, Tim and Rick."

"And which one lives here?"

Tina pointed at me.

The cop pointed at John. "What's his name?"

"John."

The cop pointed at Tim. "What's his name?"

"Tim."

The cop quickly pointed back at John, trying to trip her up.

"What's his name?"

"John."

The cop frowned. "All right miss, have a good day. C'mon fellas, let's go down." You knew he wanted to say "downtown" but "down" was as close as a housing cop was going to get.

We all got back in the elevator. The cop pressed the "L" button. He sneered at us. "You know and I know and you know I know you guys are full of it. I don't know what you were doing here but..."

"Listen you punk," John said, poking a finger in his chest. "I'm old enough to be your father! Treat me with some goddamn respect!" John gave him a serious eyeball fucking.

I'm thinking holy shit, this cop is gonna bust us now, I'm so screwed! I told you I had a quarter ounce of coke in my pocket, right? But wouldn't you know it, John was so damned intimidating the cop backed down. "Yes sir, you're right, I'm sorry."

John continued glaring at him the rest of the way down. As soon as the elevator door opened the cop scurried off, tail between his legs.

"Jesus Christ Johnny you're gonna give me a heart attack! You know I'm holding!"

John laughed. "Fuck that little bitch, somebody had to teach him some manners."

John didn't take shit from anybody. Course nowadays the cop probably would have just shot him.

And here I am, all these years later, I'm still holding, still a bust waiting to happen and I still didn't have John's nerve and I'm kowtowing to a cow town Keystone cop.

"Yessir."

"I thought I told you to be quiet, now didn't I? Look, here's what happened: You were driving down Miller and you were sure everyone was turning left and you thought you had an all-clear, is that right? Don't say anything, just nod if you understand me."

I nodded.

"Great. I'll be back in a minute." Justin took my license and registration and went back to his bike. He came back in 15 minutes and handed me a ticket. "That's a moving violation, good for two points on your license. I recommend you attend traffic school and it won't get reported to your insurance company."

The ticket was for $515. I guess somebody has to pay for Justin to ride around on his bike all day. Good thing I had a job.

As I was saying before I so rudely interrupted myself, Justin was, like most cops, a son of a bitch. The kids I knew back in high school who became cops were bullies and petty thieves, the same guys who took bets on football, sold weed and would break into cars in the school parking lot and steal stereos. But it seemed like the ones in Marin were particularly rude. Maybe it's because they're so bored. Police really don't have much to do in our little hamlet. A typical Mill Valley crime wave: a cellphone is stolen from a car. The distraught victim contacts the authorities. Law enforcement arrives and then the poor sap realizes she left the phone in her other Mercedes. Or perhaps a noise complaint: a raucous senior-citizen drum circle in the redwoods. The gray heads promise to stop drumming at 10:00 p.m. and the heat leaves them be. Or the poor 5-year-old whose bike was stolen by stoned teenagers who rode it around acting stupid until they got tired and left it at the 7-11, where the cops found it a few hours later. Or those real thuggish brats who popped BMW medallions off of hoods so they could wear them around their necks and pretend they were rappers.

Bored stiff, the local law is adamant about enforcing minor traffic violations. Who knew what they'd do if an actual major crime occurred?

As Justin walked away, I crumpled up the ticket and shoved it in the glove box, a false show of bravado as I'd most certainly take it out later and pay it. Still, it made me feel better for a moment, and that's what life is all about, isn't it? An occasional brief respite from the daily grind, even if we're just kidding ourselves and know it and aren't really fooling ourselves even for a second. I put my car in gear and continued heading downtown to the office.

  I pulled into my usual spot next to the Baskin Robbins and exited the car. To my surprise, here came Justin again, roaring in just behind me. Again with the siren? What now?

Chapter 7

Did Justin forget part of his lecture? Did he want to give me another ticket for not paying my ticket yet, or for crumpling it up? Maybe he was just lonely? He jumped off his bike and strode purposefully towards me.

"Mr. Davies? Do you have a minute?"

How did he know my name? Oh wait, that's right, it was on the ticket he'd just given me.

"Uh, sure officer." I was wondering why he was acting polite all of a sudden. I didn't like it.

"OK, hold on a second." He picked up his radio mike and spoke into it. His hand muffled his words and I couldn't understand what he was saying. Then the thing squawked, honked and buzzed back at him and he said "10-4" and disconnected.

Justin took in the storefront, saw the large block letters spelling out Charles le Chauve Realty Corp. He jerked a thumb at it. "This your office?"

"Yeah."

"Can we wait inside? The detectives will be here any minute." He smiled at me while asking, yet somehow I got the feeling he was dying to take out his truncheon and beat the snot out of me.

"Sure." Detectives? Now what? Charlie's 450SL wasn't in her reserved spot. Apparently she was taking the rest of the day off. Why not? Business was booming, just not for us. Reputation is a hard thing to recover. Justin followed me inside. I sat behind my desk while he stood gazing out the storefront's plate glass window. I didn't have a smartphone yet so I examined my fingernails and wondered why the cops wanted to talk to me; I thought the whole Ross mess was behind me, or at least I hoped it was. I'd lost the investors' bankroll, but I hadn't done anything illegal. Technically. I hoped.

The old-fashioned bell attached to the door rang as two bulls—one tall and beefy, the other short, wearing a coffee-stained trenchcoat—strolled in like they owned the place. They simultaneously took out their wallets and flashed their badges. The short rumpled one said, "Detective Keyes." He nodded at the tall one, a sandy-haired palooka with pale gray eyes. "That's my partner, Detective McGee." McGee scowled.

"Rick Davies. How can I help you, detectives?"

"Do you know a woman named Marjorie Khan?" Keyes asked, perching on the corner of my desk, making himself comfortable. He smelled like cheap cigars. Here I thought I was the only guy in Marin who wore a sport coat during the day, but Keyes had one too, though mine was a Zegna and his looked like it came off the $9.99 rack at the San Rafael Goodwill store and hadn't been dry cleaned or ironed since. He leaned in, friendly and smiling. Meanwhile McGee paced silently about the office. McGee unnerved me, which I suppose was the point, the way he was poring over every object in sight, the books on the shelves, Charlie's kids' trophies for attending soccer camp, the MLS listings posted on the wall, like he was tossing the joint, searching for a murder weapon. His nonchalance was more menacing than Keyes' attempt to act menacing.

While Justin and I had been waiting for the detectives to show up, I thought of all the things they might want to talk to me about, so I was relieved when Keyes asked me about somebody I hadn't heard of. "Marjorie Khan? No, can't say that I do, officer. What's this got to do with me?"

"I'll ask the questions here, if you don't mind."

See? What did I tell you about cops? Why do you think they call them "dicks"?

Keyes crinkled his brow, pulled a small notebook from his breast pocket and peered at it intently, like he was having trouble remembering how to read. The notebook was rumpled, too. He glimpsed up. "I understand you've got a new client, a Ms. Octavia Papadopolous, is that correct?"

"Yessir." Hmmm, just the like the housing cop in the elevator back in the day, a sudden change of subject. Was he trying to trick me?

"And you spell that p-a-p-a-d-o-p-o-l-o-u-s?"

"Most of the time. Sometimes I get mixed up and swap an 'a' for an 'o', and nobody notices, but yeah, that's pretty much it."

He scrawled something on his pad. He stared at the top of my forehead while he spoke, instead of in my eye, a classic intimidation technique. "And how are things going with selling her house? You think it will move quickly?"

Now he was doing some real detective work. A regular brain trust they have on the force. I once heard they actually won't let you join up if you have a high IQ. Proof: last week I'd been in the city, there was a band of cops standing around an elevator bank. Now, due to some quirk of human nature, most folks, when they see other people waiting at an elevator, even if the up button is lit, they go and press it anyway, as if to say to the other people waiting there, "maybe you pressed the button and the light came on, but I still don't think you know what you're doing, here, let me show you how it's done." But this time, the button wasn't lit, the cops were just standing around chatting, so I strolled over and pressed the up button and the light came on and they all went "Ahhhh!" like I'd done some sort of amazing magic trick like pull a quarter out from behind their ear.

"What's up with all the sudden interest in an old house for sale, officer? You in the market? There's never been a better time to buy."

"Like I could afford Mill Valley. Heh, we're barely managing with our little house in Richmond. We finally took the plunge last year, got a nice 3/2 for $650,000."

I whistled long and low. "Nice going, detective! It'll be worth three times that much in a few years." Ended up more like a third, but who knew?

He smiled despite himself. "That's what we're thinking. OK, we're good for the time being, Mr. Davies." Keyes flipped his notepad closed with authority. Officious prick. He turned to go but just as he was approaching the door, he spun around. "Oh yeah, just one more thing—why do you think Ms. Khan would have your business card?"

Ah, the old *Columbo* routine. I shrugged. "Beats me. I leave 'em all over town to drum up business. Like I said, I never met her. What's the big deal with how she got my card? Who is Marjorie Khan anyway?

"We found Ms. Khan's body this morning on a Homestead Valley trail. Your card was in her pocket."

Chapter 8

"We'll get back to you if we need anything else. Take care now." Justin opened the door for him and Keyes ambled out. McGee spoke for the first time, "Don't leave town. And have a nice day."

"You too, officer." Right out of a bad '70s TV show.

It was only quarter of drink o'clock, but a police interrogation is as good an excuse as any to cheat. I plopped down in my Aeron and opened the bottom drawer of my steel tanker desk and got my bottle of Maker's Mark. I'd heard it was the finest brand of bourbon in the world, I think I read that in an Elmore Leonard book, so I figured I'd try it. I didn't like it. Like all bourbon, it was terrible, but Maker's Mark was even worse because it was expensive. But what was I going to do, throw it out? I poured myself a stiff one and threw it down. It was disgusting, sickly sweet. However, my headache, which had started to return shortly after my initial contact with Justin and only grew worse after my encounter with the detectives, disappeared just like that and my aching back didn't ache so much any more. Bourbon's not so bad.

Now that I was a little lubricated, I could face Charlie. Not face to face, but on the phone. She picked up on the first ring.

"Charles le Chauve, how can I help you?" We'd tightened our pursestrings, and pretended our cellphones were business lines. Nowadays everybody does it, but back then it was a cheap trick.

"Hey Charlie it's me, Rick."

"Oh."

"Yeah, weirdest thing just happened. Couple of peace officers stopped by, giving me the second degree about a Ms. Marjorie Khan. You know her?"

"Yes, she's the owner of the house you're selling."

"Come again?"

"The house you're trying to sell, I signed the paperwork with Ms. Khan last week, and gave her your card since you're the agent she'll be working with."

"I never heard from her, just from a Ms. Papadopolous."

"You know how these estate sales go. Ownership is transferred to avoid taxes, but the actual owner isn't around or else not responsible enough to handle it, so an adult takes over."

"Yeah. Or else they're dead."

"What?"

"Turns out somebody bumped off Ms. Khan on a hiking trail. They found her body this morning. My business card in her pocket."

"That is very unfortunate news. But don't worry—the contract is still valid. Just continue working with Mrs. Papadopolous. And I wouldn't say anything to her about Marjorie Khan. I don't know if she was a relative or a friend or just an employee, but it's none of our business, savvy?"

"Gotcha. OK, thanks Charlie, that's one mystery cleared up."

She hung up, without saying goodbye or you're welcome.

I locked up the office and headed back to my home in the canyons behind downtown. I loved it back there, it was like some magical woodland kingdom, big old houses that looked like listing ships, with footbridges to their doors, scattered amongst densely packed redwood groves. You drive around one of those big old heritage redwoods half blocking West Blithedale and you expect a hobbit to peek out from behind the bole. Some folks don't like it, think it's too damp and cold in the winter. They're right, it is. It's also too damp and cold in the summer—but everywhere else in Marin always seemed too hot for me. Except of course in the summer, when it was too cold. People in San Rafael thought the weather in Mill Valley was horrible, and people in Mill Valley thought the weather in San Francisco was horrible, and people in San Francisco thought the weather on the East Coast was horrible. As Mark Twain once said, if you don't like the weather in San Francisco, go fuck yourself. Maybe not those exact words, but close enough.

When I first came out to Marin and was house hunting, a friend who had been living here for a long time told me to avoid the canyons, because they had a bad microclimate. Microclimates, huh. Hoo-boy—I'm in woo-woo California all right. And not just California, but Marin County. Where nobody will make a real estate purchase without consulting their kinesiologist, the Jews are all Buddhists, Okies two generations from the Dust Bowl pretend they're WASPs, and people seriously believe in microclimates. Turns out, the microclimate thing, silly and new-agey as it sounded, is for real. Some summer days I'd wake up in the morning, look out the back window and see the fog rolling over the hill, poking some exploratory tendrils down into the gullies and creeks, like a giant misty squid. Most of the time, the fog's tentacles would retreat as the sun advanced higher in the sky, burning off by 11 or noon. Other days, the marine layer would keep advancing, swooping down the valley like something out of a John Carpenter movie, and the sky would be slate gray all day, the air would be moist and 55 degrees. In July. And you could get in your car, drive north over the hill to Corte Madera and it would be 82 and sunny. But the other way, the south side of that hill, where the fog came from every morning, that was Tam Valley, and it was foggy there every day all summer. Which was why houses there cost 20% less than they did on this side of the hill, in Mill Valley proper, and Mrs. P and all the other NIMBYs looked down their nose at its denizens.

I had barely driven out of my office parking lot when it happened, at the stop sign where Miller meets Sunnyside, right before The Depot. A beat-up red pickup truck, gardening gear overflowing out of its bed, was slowing to a stop in front of me, when its side-view mirror brushed against a bicyclist passing them on the right. The cyclist fell to the ground.

I watched as two Hispanic guys, dressed in grass-stained work clothes, jumped out of the truck and went to check on the biker, who was now struggling to get back on his feet. The gardeners moved over to help him—that's what it looked like to me, but eyewitness accounts would later differ, as they always do. Some insisted the landscapers meant to give the bike rider a beat-down from the jump. The cyclist got back up and smacked one of the landscapers upside the head with his U-Lock.

The poor sap clutched his noggin and dropped like a sack of potatoes. The second gardener held up his hands, palms outward, yelling, *"Càlmate, Càlmate!"* which I believe is Mexican for "Hey, dude, chill out!" The bicyclist, decked head to foot in skin-tight, bright yellow Spandex, like some swell in the Tour de France, did a Billy Jack and kicked the guy in the jaw. It was like somebody gave Krav Maga lessons to a giant canary.

I didn't want to get involved. Where the heck was Justin now that we needed him? The bike rider started kicking the landscaper—I wasn't sure if it was the first or the second one. I sighed, pressed the button to turn off my Beemer and stepped out.

"Yo Buddy, what the hell?"

"Mind your own business!" shouted the cyclist.

I walked toward him. "Dude, whatever happened here, even if those guys hit you, you can't just beat them up here in the middle of the street."

"No? Watch me." He switched to the other guy, kicking him in the ribs. Both gardeners rolled on the street, moaning. I took out my Treo and began to dial 911 when two cruisers, a county sheriff and a highway patrol, came out of nowhere and screeched to a halt. Four flatfoots jumped out. I expected them to have pistols drawn in a violent situation like this, but then I remembered the perp was a rich white guy.

"OK pal, you better quit now," I said.

"Yeah, Jesus," the biker said, dusting off his Spandex. "I don't know what came over me." He took a deep breath and combed his Gordon

Gecko-style slicked-back hair with his fingers.

"You all right there dude?"

"No! I'm a wreck. See, I run a tech startup, late stage, we had 400 employees, locations in London, Sydney, New York, Toronto. We were supposed to do an IPO later this year," he said as the cops approached.

Why was he telling me all this? It's not like I was making $275 an hour standing in the road while this maniac yuppie spilled his guts.

"Obviously that's not happening now. I'm down to just one office, in the city, 20 employees hanging on for dear life. No cash to make payroll this month. I don't even bother going in anymore. I'm completely fucked."

Thank goodness the cops arrived so I didn't have to listen to any more of this sad sack's sob story. Smiling, one of the sheriffs said, "Good afternoon sir, how are you?" as he gently guided the cyclist's hands behind his back and cuffed him. The psycho biker didn't protest or fight back or try to explain himself. The gardeners were still on the ground, groaning.

As the sheriffs took him back to their car, the cyclist turned back to me and said, "Hey bro, can you do me a solid and take my bike for me? That thing's custom, cost me twelve grand."

Why do I constantly find myself in these situations? I guess I just have a friendly face. "Uh, sure, man, how will I get it back to you?"

"Don't worry, I'll find you," he said as the sheriff laid a hand on his crown and stuffed him into the back seat of the cruiser. They drove off.

The highway patrol guy loomed over the landscapers, chewing on a toothpick, eyes hidden behind mirrored glasses. "You OK?"

"*Si, señor,* uh, yes," one said. He was older looking than the other one and had a Pancho Villa mustache. "*Vamonos,*" he said to the younger one, probably his son or nephew, as he helped him off the ground.

The cop put a hand on the older one's shoulder. "You boys got ID?"

Nobody paid me any mind as I picked up the $12,000 bicycle and tossed it in my trunk. I drove around the red pickup as the highway patrolman called his partner over and arrested the landscapers.

Chapter 9

I parked in front of my house and trundled up the 39 stone steps (yes, I've counted them). Carrying some stranger's expensive bike didn't make it any easier. I entered the kitchen, sweaty, huffing and puffing, and poured myself a water tumbler of Laphroaig. I was glad to be home, and I deserved the good stuff. I thought about working on my novel. Letting my imagination take over after a rough day helps me relax, especially after filling up with top-shelf writing fluid.

The story takes place in a near-future, apocalyptic New York. A character based on Donald Trump rules the city with an iron fist. He seals off midtown Manhattan with a giant wall, and lets peons from the outer boroughs enter his fortress to do menial labor. Once a week, he and his Eastern European wife throw food scraps off of their balcony to the starving masses below in lieu of paychecks. Then everything changes when a giant alien spaceship shows up, just like Ronald Reagan's fantasy. They randomly pick some junkie loser out of the crowd to be the new ruler of Earth. Speaking of Ronald Reagan, he's still the President, even though he would be well over 100 years old. Nobody knows if he's a body double or a robot or what, but they don't care—everybody loves Reagan and is happy he's still in charge. I'd been working on my magnum opus, on and off, for almost 20 years. The plot had some kinks to work out, and the characters were underdeveloped, but I was committed.

I decided to watch TV instead. I sunk into my Eames lounge chair—not one of those cheap online knockoffs, the real deal. And not the off-the-rack black leather and walnut, I have the one with the Oiled Santos Palisander veneer and cream Vicenza leather, usually an extra two grand, but I'd done a favor for the guy over at the Design Within Reach on

Miller and he'd let me have it at the annual sale price, only 3.5k. The chair was incredibly comfortable, and every time I succumbed to its ergonomic charms I relaxed even more knowing I'd gotten a deal.

Deeply reclined, I sipped at my high-end Scotch and watched an episode of *Lost* on my almost-new 37" Panasonic plasma. The picture was fantastic, sharp and bright, the blacks deep yet detailed, but it didn't help the show, which had jumped the shark. Or maybe it had always sucked and I just hadn't noticed till now. Move the island? And who is this Richard Alpert guy who keeps visiting Locke? Wasn't he Timothy Leary's "research" partner back in the day? Mildly disgusted at myself for wasting my time on this nonsense—if there's one thing I hate, it's pointless, poorly structured tales that rely on shock value to maintain your interest—I switched off the boob tube and put on a CD, *Mingus at Antibes*, retreated to my comfy chair and picked up the book I was reading, *Double Indemnity*. I'd already read it three or four times, but not for awhile, so I was enjoying it again.

My eyes grew heavy and I put the book down for a minute. I was dead tired and I felt my consciousness start to fade to black. It occurred to me that the awareness you have of falling asleep, the sensation of ego dissipation, is probably how it feels when you die. I love falling asleep, so maybe dying isn't so bad. Not that I'm in any hurry to find out.

"Hey bro, what's up?"

Barney stood at the foot of the ottoman, clutching a hammer. Confused, I propped myself up on my elbows and leaned forward.

"Barney?" I rubbed my eyes. "The fuck you doing here?"

"Well, you know me, I got a ton of things I gotta take care of, but I wanted to check in with you and see how you're doing."

I was perplexed. "Me? I'm fine, I guess." I reached over to the side table and put on my rimless glasses, which I'm too vain to wear during the day. I wondered if I should get that Lasik surgery. I felt somehow detached from myself, like I wasn't fully awake and sure of my identity yet.

I blinked but still had sand in my eyes. Barney stood there, grinning, tool belt around his waist, knuckles wrapped white around the wooden handle of the hammer. This was disturbing. I tried to think of what I'd done to piss him off. "Barney, whaddya gonna do with that hammer?"

Barney looked down and studied the hammer, surprised to see he was holding it. "This? I guess I gotta lot of work to do." He knitted his brow, puzzled. That made two of us. Now I was getting mad.

"What the hell are you doing here, anyway?" I decided to start locking my doors at night.

"I'm not sure," Barney said. He seemed confused. He looked at his feet, then straight in my eye. "Rick, do you like me?"

Somehow, this didn't seem like a peculiar question, so it didn't feel strange to answer honestly. "Actually Barney, not really. I think you're a pussy. The way you let your ex walk all over you? Paying her rent even though she has a job and a live-in boyfriend? I mean, you're not a bad guy, I guess I just don't have any respect for you."

Barney pursed his lips, taking it in stride. "Yeah, I gotcha. OK, well I'm outta here. See you around." He disappeared and I fell back into the soft leather cushions.

Now my cellphone was buzzing, loudly. My head hurt. I really shouldn't have had that third glass of Scotch, but how else was I gonna make it through that crappy show? The sun streamed in mercilessly. A really cool, penetrating bass line played over and over again. The Mingus CD was skipping. Remember when they told us CDs lasted forever, and would never skip? I should have kept my vinyl, but I guess I needed the bread for coke at the time. Hey, how else are you supposed to spend your youth if you don't misspend it? I groped, found my phone.

"Hello?" I said, still half asleep and sounding like Miles Davis.

"Hey Rick?"

"Yeah?"

"Hey man, it's me, Dobbs."

"Dobbs? What's up?"

"You hear about Barney?"

Uh-oh. "No man, what happened?"

"You're sitting down, right?"

"Dobbs, it's like—" I glanced at the time on my Treo. It was 7:22 a.m. "—fucking dawn and shit. And yeah, I am sitting down." Dobbs seemed like a total dim bulb sometimes, or spaced out, a wet brain, but he also had an uncanny sixth sense, like he knew I had passed out in my chair. I was surprised he was up, then realized he probably hadn't gone to bed yet.

"Oh cool, right on." I didn't say anything and Dobbs didn't either. Then he spoke. "Barney died last night."

"Huh? What? What happened?" I sat up. Now I was wide awake.

"Dunno." I could practically hear Dobbs shrugging his shoulders over the phone. "The neighbors found him—they were pissed off 'cause he was listening to a record really loud and it kept skipping. They peeked in his window and saw him collapsed, draped over a big antique dresser. They're thinking he had a heart attack lifting the thing."

Collapsed on the dresser? That fuckin' guy, he was supposed to bring it to my house, not his. Wait, wasn't he here last night? The cobwebs cleared. No, that's right, he wasn't. I don't think. "Damn! I mean, he was a young guy." Just a few years old than me, I thought.

"I know, bummer right?" Dobbs sounded nonchalant, but I guess he'd lost a lot of people over the years. Occupational hazard. "Barney had heart problems."

"I didn't know."

"Me neither, but apparently he had some a those, whaddya call 'em, stents, which is not a good sign I guess for a guy in his fifties. But he still kept smoking and I think he did drugs sometimes too." Dobbs laughed, but not in a cruel way, more as if to say, "Can you freakin' believe I'm still alive?"

Dobbs had probably done as much acid as anyone on the planet, and more than his share of the hard stuff too. "Barney had his faults, like we all do. But he had his good points too, right?"

"Sure, I guess so." Then it hit me. I felt a lump in my throat. "Look man I gotta go, let me know if you hear anything else." I hung up before Dobbs could say another word, or, even worse, before I said anything to implicate myself. Holy snap! I gave Barney a freakin' eight ball! I didn't know about the stents, or any health problems, I just knew Barney liked his yayo. Me, I liked it once upon a time, now I can't stand the stuff, makes me all jangly. I need to calm down, not get worked up. I was sick to my stomach; how much trouble was I in? I ran my hands through my hair. My hair is nice and thick. I still have pretty good hair for a guy my age. I heard a knock at the door.

Chapter 10

I debated whether to ignore the knock, but then it came again, louder, more insistent. I glanced down at my Treo: 7:45 a.m. Dammit. Who would come calling for me at this ungodly hour? Must be the cops, they've figured out I'm the one who gave the coke to Barney. Better get my story straight.

I hurriedly slipped on some track pants, threw on a t-shirt and my slip-on Merrells. I remembered from *Bonfire of the Vanities* that you had to dress right when you went to jail. They take away your belt and your shoelaces, so you want pants with an elastic waist band, so they don't fall to your knees (which is how the droopy-drawers fashion trend originated) and shoes without laces, so your shoes don't fall off after they take your laces away so you can't hang yourself. The knock came again.

"Awright, awright, I'm coming," I shouted. I was relieved to see my downstairs neighbor Sean through the glass panels of the door. Which is not how I usually felt when I saw Sean, because he is an annoying asshole. OK, now you're thinking but Rick, you're kind of an asshole too; maybe you have a point, but at least I know I'm an asshole, while Sean was oblivious to that fact. Anyway, at that moment I was relieved to see him instead of Five-0. Sean lived in the garden apartment below me, and he came by frequently—but never a social call. He would stop over to complain about noise: if I watched TV too loud, or played music at any volume, or if a girl I was with got overexuberant, or if I was just walking around after 10:00 p.m. and the floors squeaked. Sometimes, to change it up a bit, he complained that I parked too close to his spot and he didn't have room for his ridiculous gargantuan Yukon, the gas guzzler they named after the part of Canada they had to destroy to slake its insatiable thirst for hydrocarbons. And yes, of course it had a "Keep Tahoe Blue" bumper sticker. Did you really have to ask? And a second bumper sticker: "Please God, just one more bubble!" Sean could be here to complain about any of these things, or to voice a different complaint I hadn't heard yet. But since it was early in the morning, it was more likely Sean needed something. That was the other time he called, when he was looking for a favor. Sean was either surly, pissed off, and self-righteous, or else friendly with a big smile and a "Hey man, can I borrow an iPod charger?" or "Can you help me carry a desk up the stairs?" or "Can I use your washer and dryer to do a couple of loads?"

But I was glad to see Sean instead of the police. Sort of. "What can I do ya for, neighbor?" I asked, doing my best Ned Flanders to pre-emptively lighten the mood.

The *Simpsons* reference went right over Sean's head. Either he was too busy to follow pop culture, or, more likely, he didn't pay attention when others spoke. He had that conversational technique of powerful (or just self-involved) people, who look you right in your peepers when they speak to you, but when you respond their eyes dart off to the side, like they're constantly scouring the horizon, on the lookout for somebody more important than you. I wasn't sure what he did for a living, something in finance. Sean lived up in Tahoe, the Nevada side, with his family and used the garden studio as a pied-à-terre, a stepping stone on his way to SFO for his frequent travels back East. He got all his mail here, and asked me to pick it up for him. As if I didn't have enough to do already. Had to be some kind of tax dodge. He was only in town three or four days a month, which is why he didn't drive me completely batty.

"Dude, this is so messed up. The Yuke won't start? And I've got a super-important meeting in the city in 45 minutes?"

I knew what was coming, but still couldn't believe it. These were the pre-Uber times, and friends would actually lend a friend their car if they had to. But Sean was not my friend.

"Can you be a bro and borrow me your Beemer? Just for a few hours, and I'll owe you super big time."

Sean must have figured he had nothing to lose by asking me, of all people, for such a boon, so his jaw dropped when I shrugged, dug in my pocket and threw him the keys. "Bring it back in one piece, or I'll have to track you down and kill you."

Sean laughed. "Dude! You're the best!" He high-tailed it down the 39 steps before I could change my mind, which was probably a good idea, as I was already wondering why I'd done it. Probably 'cause I was just so grateful he wasn't Johnny Law, I'd have said yes to just about anything.

I was somehow pleased with myself, as if I'd outsmarted Sean, even though, if anything, it was the other way around. Then I remembered, as I heard my car roar off, the brokers' open was tomorrow. How the hell was I going to get to the old lady's house to prepare? I pulled my Treo out of my pocket, ready to call Sean and renege on the favor, but realized I didn't have his number. Because, like, why would I ever want to call him? Come to think of it, now that Barney was dead, who was going to get the old lady's place painted and cleaned up on such short notice?

I was hungover, tired, scared, confused, in over my head. The solution was obvious: the guy who woke me up this morning, Dobbs. Dobbs had been living in this town for 40 years or so, everybody knew him, and he knew everybody. If anybody could help me out now, it was Dobbs. I opened my Treo, looked up Dobbs' number, pressed it with the stylus.

"Huh? Whuzzat?"

"Hey Dobbs, it's me, Rick."

"Oh Rick, man, how you doing? Man, you hear about Barney?"

"Uh, yeah, you called me and told me the news a few minutes ago, remember?"

"I did? Wow, I guess I been calling so many people I can't keep 'em straight. Or maybe I just fell asleep and dreamed I called them. Well, at least I won't call you agin now. Unless I forget agin."

Dobbs sounded half in the bag, maybe even three-quarters. Then again, Dobbs seemed out of it ever since he blew his mind out during the Summer of Love. It was 8:00 a.m., but like I said, 8:00 a.m. doesn't mean the same to Dobbs as it does to you and me. If he was really partying, he was just getting into high gear. I sometimes envied him, wished I was rich and semi-famous, not give two spurts what anybody thought, get drunk whenever I felt like it. No job to get in the way of all the hot-and-cold running girls. Some consider Dobbs' lifestyle decadent, spiritually meaningless, empty. But if that was empty, I'd sure like to see what full looked like. Hell, I'd like to give half empty a try.

"Dobbs, I need help."

"What is it man? Anything for you, Rick."

I had done Dobbs a big favor once, way back when I first arrived in California and had a shitty gig working for Bill Graham Productions. Actually it was my ex did him the favor, I just gave her permission to help him out. It's complicated. Anyway, that's neither here nor there. But Dobbs knew that I actually cared for him, unlike so many starfuckers and fanboys who'd suck up to him then make fun of him behind his back, who thought he was a joke of a person. Say what you wanted about Dobbs, he was loyal and he never forgot when somebody did right by him. And, even if he couldn't sing for shit, he was a pretty good guitar player.

"You still renovating?"

Dobbs laughed. "Dude, it's like the fuckin' Winchester mansion over here. My old lady's got a lot of ideas, wants to try 'em all out. Then she changes her mind."

"I hear you. Look, I'm in a jam, what with Barney being, uh, out of the picture. Can you lend me your crew for the day today? I've got to put some lipstick on a pig, pronto. Brokers' open, tomorrow."

"Yeah man, I'll make it happen. By the way, we're gonna have a memorial for Barney Saturday at the Unitarian Church in San Rafael. You know it, the place on the hill, looks like Noah's ark?"

"Yeah, sure, I'll be there. Boy, you work fast, I can't believe how quick you got that set up."

"I've had plenty of practice, man."

He wasn't kidding. His band went through keyboard players like Spinal Tap went through drummers. "Oh yeah, one more thing—can you give me a lift?" I made my confession, admitted the most embarrassing thing a Californian can: "I don't have a car."

Chapter 11

Dobbs picked me up in his Ferrari 20 minutes later. I think he was glad to have an excuse to avoid trying to sleep. He was dressed, as usual, like a bum. His beard was getting grayer, longer and increasingly matted. He didn't have the mien you'd expect of your typical Ferrari driver.

The Ferrari experience is strange. You're essentially laying down, with your neck bent and your head poking up like a prairie dog, your butt not more than a few inches off the ground. It's like being in a really fast go-cart while somebody runs a vacuum cleaner next to your head. It's just plain silly in town, where you don't dare go more than a few miles over the 30 mph speed limit. But rich middle-aged men want to buy the cars they lusted after and couldn't afford when they were young. Bully for them.

The car chugged along, sputtering loudly, feeling like a angry bulldog held back by a choker chain. It needed a tune-up. "Sorry I have to pick you up in this piece of shit, I gotta take it out once a week or it stops working. You know what 'Ferrari' stands for?"

"No, what?"

"Fix It Again, Tony."

As Dobbs drove me over to the old lady's house, he spoke animatedly about the Tao of physics, black holes, the CIA's LSD mind control experiments, HAARP, stuff like that. Dobbs could barely read—he had a bad case of dyslexia—so this esoteric mish-mash he was laying on me was stuff he'd picked up from cable-TV documentaries, sci-fi movies, *Coast to Coast AM*, and late-night rap sessions with other stoned musicians. It didn't make much sense, not to me, at least. But neither did anything else these days, and he was nice enough to give me a ride, so I listened politely, inserting a "Really? That's wild!" or a "Wow!" at appropriate junctures, while he informed me about UFOs, chemtrails and how jet fuel can't melt steel beams. A laugh a minute.

We parked in front of the spooky ramshackle house and Dobbs was now in full-on output-only mode, rapping a mile a minute. I didn't even try to get a placeholder word in edgewise, so I stared out the window as he rattled on. "Martin Luther King? They proved the government assassinated him in a court of law, man! I know what I'm talkin' about, I've been to the owl camp at Bohemian Grove!" As we pulled up, four smiling, five-foot-tall Guatemalan guys approached the car and Dobbs gave them the thumbs up. I told Dobbs thanks for everything and crawled out of the Ferrari.

"Hang on a sec." He reached into the jump seat and handed me a backpack. "I have a feeling you could use this. I don't need it anymore, I'm on the wagon."

"Oh man, thank you! You're the best!" I didn't know what was in the bag, but whatever it was, I was pretty sure I was going to like it. A lot.

He peeled out and shouted something over his shoulder, something about how I shouldn't worry about getting the house ready in time because the universe was a hologram and time didn't exist and…but his voice was lost in the squeal of the tires and rumble of the engine and I missed the last part.

I told Dobbs' guys I'd pay them $20 an hour till dark, then $30 for as long as they could go after that, and I slipped them each an extra double sawbuck to get started. They liked that, and were soon slapping on paint, sweeping, replacing rugs and polishing floors like gangbusters. While they slogged away, I spent the day on the phone, making sure every realtor in the county knew about tomorrow's open house. I had to tell the Guatemalans to quit at midnight; they would have gone till dawn if I'd let them, but I was bushed and far be it for me to let the good suffer in search of perfection.

The house didn't look new by any means, but it was neat as a pin. The stagers had come by in the evening. The old lady's nasty old furniture was gone, as were the cats. The house didn't smell like it had feline bladder issues anymore. It seemed good to me, at 1:00 a.m., in dim light, when I was at the bottom of a wine bottle. Whether it would pass muster in the bright of day, when I was sober, might be another story. But you could say the same about me, so I didn't worry about it.

I hadn't meant to polish off the whole bottle Dobbs gave me. Shit, I hadn't meant to open it at all, it was a Haut Brion 2001, and I thought I should save it for a special occasion. You don't open a $400 bottle of wine for no reason. But Barney was dead, no cops had bothered me today, and, against all odds, I'd gotten the old lady's place ready for the brokers' open tomorrow. So a little celebration was due. Why not get stinko on the good stuff? I couldn't always get it, or have the dough for it, but I always wanted the best. Second best sucks—it means somebody else somewhere got what was rightfully yours. It's like they're mocking you. Anything less than the very best leaves me with an empty feeling, a gaping void of deep dissatisfaction felt in the pit of my stomach. So, Haut Brion it was. Who's laughing now?

I was fooling myself. Haut Brion 2001 is excellent vino. *Wine Spectator* gives it a 96, saying "Intense aromas of violets, berries and spices follow through to a full-bodied palate, with layers of super silky tannins and a long, long finish." But Robert Parker, even though he describes it as having "an unmistakable nobility as well as a burgeoning complexity" and reveals "pure notes of sweet and sour cherries, black currants, licorice, smoke, and crushed stones," still only gives it a 94. Excellent vino. But not the best. Someday I hoped to be able to buy the stuff Dobbs drinks, $20,000 bottles of Domaine de la Romanee-Conti Grand Cru. (Dobbs isn't supposed to be drinking at all—he tells his friends and family he's in AA—but I guess really good wine doesn't count. Maybe the Haut Brion wasn't good enough for him to not consider it a relapse. It's nice to have rich friends.)

I lay down on a brand-new antique chaise lounge for a minute to clear my head. I plugged in my $500 Etymotic earbuds and spun my iPod wheel to 7/18/76, one of my all-time favorites. Nothing like a "Lazy St. Stephen" on the Travis Bean. So intense yet so relaxing at the same time. '76 is totally underrated. The next thing I knew I heard a loud pounding, Bam! Bam! Bam! I was confused, I wasn't sure where I was, or even who I was, and I couldn't tell if the noise was coming from outside or inside my head. I opened my eyes and realized I'd passed out on a comfy chair, two days in a row now. Apparently I was on a roll.

"Hello, anybody home? Caterers!"

Damn. Well, at least I'd managed to sleep the whole night through without having to get up to piss, after all that wine, so I had that going for me.

I yelled at the door, "Uh, c'mon in, it's open, I'll be right with you." I skulked over to the bathroom, each step on the Pottery Barn fake Persian rug feeling like a nail gun to the back of my head. You know what they say, about good wine not giving you a hangover? They're lying.

I splashed cold water on my face, ran wet fingers through my hair. My hair hurt and my fingers felt puffy. The freshly cleaned sink and bathroom were bare. Nothing worse than seeing used toiletry articles in the bathroom when you were thinking of buying a house. OK, a shit stain in the toilet bowl was worse. But not much.

I looked at my Treo until my eyes focused. Eleven o'clock! Stupid caterers were supposed to have been here at 10:00 a.m., but instead made me oversleep. Thanks to their irresponsibility and poor work ethic, now I didn't even have time to go home and shower and shave. I opened the medicine cabinet and lo and behold, there was a rolled-up travel-size tube of toothpaste that Dobbs' crew had missed. I'd have to have a word with them about their oversight. I unscrewed the cap, rolled up the tube as far as it would go and was able to squeeze out a tiny dollop of toothpaste onto my fingertip. I rubbed my teeth with the hard, gritty stuff, trying not to think of how old it must have been. I was reminded of the story of the couple moving out of the place they'd been living in for decades. In a stack of boxes jammed into a corner of their garage that they'd meant to put away ages ago but had never gotten around to, they found their lost pet tortoise, who'd gone missing 20 years earlier. The tortoise was hungry and glad to see them. I rinsed out and dried my mouth on my sleeve.

I slowly ambled back to the living room, now replete with Crate and Barrel and Room and Board castoffs. I could hear the caterers noisily unpacking in the kitchen. I peeked out the window. A swell-looking babe—skinny, fit, blonde—a Marin classic—was dismounting from a gigantic yellow Hummer. It could have been a shot from a Chamber of Commerce promo video—"Come to Mill Valley, where the cars are huge and the women are tiny!" She strode confidently up the newly power-washed steps, now lined on either side with fresh plantings, lavender and phormium and agapanthus, a bunch of annual flowers, all cheap highway trash we'd picked up at Home Depot, but it looked a lot better than the original crabgrass, dirt and dandelions. The plants would all be dead in a month because nobody would bother to water them, but who cared? The place would be sold long before then.

Now who was this fine specimen? Somebody I wanted to meet, of that I was sure. I ran over to the front door and opened it so she knocked on air.

"Oh, don't I look silly?"

"My bad," I said, drinking her in. She had dark, olive skin and plump, bee-stung lips, a helluva chassis and legs that went on for days. Her hair was bleached blonde but she had bushy black eyebrows. There was about as much chance the carpet matched the drapes as there is that LeBron James drives a Kia. That's what deductive reasoning told me, but I wouldn't be happy till I had empirical evidence. She reminded me of my ex, Gail, back in her prime. Although Gail still looked pretty good when I ran into her at Peet's, thanks to frequent visits to the Marin Laser Academy for Botox injections, skin rejuvenation and general barnacle scrapeage, all paid for by yours truly.

The knockout held out a small, soft hand. "Rick Davies?" Now she took a turn and gave me the once over. "My, you're a big one, aren't you?" I'm only five-foot nine, so I'm not sure what she meant.

"I've heard so much about you, how nice to finally meet." She smiled, showing perfect white teeth as she handed me an embossed business card. I stared at the card, trying to make sense of it. I was still off kilter and the tiny print was blurry but I couldn't miss the big Charles le Chauve logo. Why hadn't Charlie told me about a new hire? Why hadn't I met her?

"I'm Kirsten, and I'm here to help."

Chapter 12

"I'm sorry, you have me at a disadvantage. What now? You work for Charlie?"

"Yup! Just started today, and this is my first open." Eyes wide open, like she was trying to match the photo on her business card, or posing for a Walter Keane painting, she beamed and walked in right past me, clocking the joint, taking it all in. "I love it so far!" Then she stage whispered to me, "I really need a job, and Charlie's a doll for helping me out."

I tried to look pleased. She was not as young as I thought on first blush but was extremely well-preserved. She wore a white Chanel knockoff pantsuit that complimented her nice rack. I imagined lifting her shirt over her head and watching her boobs move up with the motion and then barely coming back down, nipples standing up at attention, looking me straight in the eye, unafraid and proud. Women readers are now thinking "What a pig!" I'm just being transparent, as we like to say out here—all red-blooded men think this way. Sorry, ladies.

"Whatever. We'll sort it out later. For now, I'm glad you're here. Look, can you cover me for a minute? I gotta run out, I forgot something at home."

"No problem, I got this. The other brokers won't be here for another 45 minutes at least if, uh, you need to, you know, do anything to get ready." She gave me a California smile, subtlely letting me know I looked like dogshit.

"Aw, thanks for understanding," I said, putting a hand on her shoulder like they tell you to do in how-to managerial books. I felt her neck and shoulder tense up, like I was George Bush and she was Angela Merkel. I took my hand away and grinned right back at her. "You're the best, Kiki."

The friendly façade dropped. "Kiki? Ugh, don't call me that, that's what my father called me."

I just met this broad and already I'm her shrink. "I'll be back by noon, I swear."

"No need to swear," she said. "Like I said, I got this." She smiled again. Or had she ever stopped smiling, since I'd first met her? She was either a genuinely happy person with a radiant sunny disposition, or else just another miserable slob who hides her depression with constant grinning and laughter. I hoped it was the former, but since she was in this business, it was probably the latter. Nobody wants to be a realtor when they grow up. When everything else has gone south, this is the business that chooses you.

"I owe ya one, kid!" I said over my shoulder as I dashed out the door, not wanting any other early-bird colleagues or competitors to witness me in such a delicate condition.

I ran out to the street and remembered I didn't have a car. My head was killing me. I wished I'd grabbed the last couple of morphine tablets from my glove box before I'd given the keys to Sean. I regretted lending Sean my car. What was I thinking? I meekly slunk back to the house.

"Hey, what's up?" asked Kirsten. She tried to furrow her brow but it wouldn't move. Botox is a helluva drug.

She was sympathetic to a fault and handed me her keys; the keychain had a whole bunch of multi-colored plastic tags on it; good luck charms, I supposed. A rabbit foot substitute for the animal-rights minded? I went back out and lifted myself up into Kirsten's yellow Hummer, a $40,000 piece of crap, a giant Tonka-toy body welded onto a $10,000 pickup truck. But I'm not one to complain. Kirsten was a good egg, I'd have to thank her somehow. Too bad I gave that whole vial of blow to Barney—I could have used a toot myself. If only I'd kept half of it, maybe Barney would have been OK. It reminded me of that old joke, if only Karen Carpenter had eaten Mama Cass's turkey sandwich, they'd both still be alive. See where generosity gets you?

I got back to my crib. No sign of Sean and my Beemer. Where the hell was he? To make matters worse, my landlord Greg's car, a Boxster, was parked in front. The Boxster is a poser mobile, a Porsche that only costs $45,000. I climbed the 39 faux-stone concrete steps to my deck, struggling for breath. Greg was about the last person I wanted to see. Never mind him, I didn't want to see anybody. I wanted to take a shower, change into some fresh clothes, have a hair of the dog, and do it all in twelve minutes. No sign of Greg; I ducked into my house.

"Hey Buddy, what's up?" Greg appeared from around the corner and stuck his shiny bald head in the doorway. "Can I come in?" By law, like a vampire, a landlord can't enter your house unless you invite him in.

"Yeah sure," I said. My head pounded, and the hike up all those stairs made me break out in a cold sweat. I hoped this would be quick. At least this was "nice" Greg, meaning he wanted a favor. Either that or else he was gonna ask me once again if I wanted to buy the house. I'd looked at the county's public records, Greg had bought the place two years ago for 905k; I signed a lease shortly thereafter. According to Zillow it had appreciated about 25% since then; they gave it a Zestimate of 1.15. It irked Greg that I was still paying the same rent as when I'd moved in.

I poured myself a glass of organic, cold-pressed orange juice, not much more than fancy flavored sugar water, but it helps with hangovers. I didn't offer him any.

"So hey guy, I'm gonna have the lawn re-seeded this week. Can you water it every day for like 15 minutes?"

"Sure," I said, not hearing what he'd said. I had things on my mind.

"When you gonna buy this house? I know you love it here."

I liked the place OK. It had a nice view, but *way* too many steps to climb up before you could enjoy it. Not really a problem unless you were carrying groceries, or it was raining, or it was dark out, or you had a bum knee or you were tired or drunk or were carrying somebody's bicycle or whatever. In other words, 90% of the time. The kitchen was tiny and needed updating ("Custom Cabinetry"). It was ostensibly a three-bedroom but one of the bedrooms was tiny, better suited as a home office. ("Cozy") The deck, which was teetering and full of splinters, was too small. The hardwood floors were sloped, so there were probably foundation issues. ("Award-Winning Seismic Retrofit!") The fireplace was non-functional and the chimney was shot. A fireplace would have been nice, as winters were brutally cold, as, like most older houses in California, there was no insulation and the windows were single-pane and drafty. ("Great Indoor-Outdoor Flow.") In the summer, the sun beat down on the cliffside house till it heated up like an EZ-Bake oven. ("Magical And Romantic Setting.") Bottom line, the place had its charms but needed a ton of work and, even when it was done, it would still have a funky layout, be at the top of four flights of stairs and not have a garage ("Easy Parking!"). The view was pretty good. The lush hillsides, a bit of the bay and the boats of Sausalito off in the distance. If you leaned way over the railing you could even catch a glimpse of San Francisco. ("Peekaboo City Views!") Not bad for a rental, but hardly sensational by local standards.

"You know it's a bargain at one and a quarter."

"Sure. But why let it go for nothing? Another year you can get one point five. You know it, I know it, everybody knows it."

Prices had gone so bananas the last few years, Greg probably could've gotten one and a quarter for the strictly B-minus house, but he was such a cheapskate he wouldn't put it on the market—he wanted me to buy it so he wouldn't have to pay the 6% broker's commission. Greed is funny. It pops up in strange ways at unexpected times, the old reptilian brain demanding its due. Like when I was a teenager and my beloved Uncle Joe passed away, I was devastated, yet the thought arose in my mind, "I wonder if I'll get his record collection?" Humans are screwed up, am I right? Anyway, it didn't matter, I was in no position to buy a house in Mill Valley, or Merced for that matter, not for one point two five, not for zero point two five, but Greg didn't need to know that.

My ruse worked. He rubbed his jaw, mulling it over. I didn't want to buy it, wouldn't if I could have, but I wanted to stay there as long as I could, so the more I delayed his selling it, the better. It occurred to me that you could turn Greg upside down and draw some lines on his chin and a big mouth on his forehead and…ah, I had to stop thinking like this. "Yeah, you're right, but I might have to raise the rent on you then."

"You gotta give me a 60-day warning, and you can only raise it 12%. And then I won't water your mother-raping lawn."

"All right, all right. I'm sensing some negative energy here, let's build bridges instead of fences, OK?" He smiled and clapped my back. "Always the businessman, you are. You shoulda been on Wall Street."

"Not my wheelhouse. But I figure I'd be doing better than those ass clowns at Bear Stearns."

"Ain't that the truth. But I'll give you a tip—pick up some Lehman stock. It's dirt cheap, and they're so tied in to the establishment, they can't let that fucker go down. Never been a better time to buy."

Chapter 13

I needed a shower even more after speaking with that unctuous mofo Greg, or at least it felt that way. While water softly yet painfully drizzled on my head, I washed down a couple of Tylenol 3s with a slug of vodka. I brushed my teeth, with a toothbrush this time, and shaved. I donned my blue Brioni suit, the best one I owned—we realtors dress up better for each other than we do for clients—and laced up my Bruno Maglis. Hangover going the way of the buffalo, I carelessly raced down the treacherous steps and mounted Kirsten's Hummer, feeling on top of the world.

I mean that literally—the damn truck was so tall I felt like I was on a motorized mountain. Metaphorically, the mountain was on top of me. I was a total loser, passing out on a lumpy faux-antique chaise lounge, making a terrible impression on a new (and hot) colleague. I'd really screwed the pooch. You'd think the poor pooch would be used to it by now. As I drove up to the old lady's house, there were so many Range Rovers, Beemers, Mercedes and Lexi I had to park half a block away. Life had been good to realtors the past few years. I took a deep breath and, determined to change my own mind, I did a quick positive visualization, a technique I'd picked up from a Tony Roberts telethon on PBS. When your thinking is foggy, go magical.

I closed my eyes at the doorstep, imagined myself rich, and felt much better. I wasn't late—I was worth waiting for. These were my people, after all, and they were here because I summoned them to see my offering. They all wanted their 1.5% cut, they wanted to work with me. I was the shit. We'd scrubbed and painted the house clean, replaced the rugs, taken out all the cat-scratched furniture and staged it beautifully. The hors d'oeuvres were locartisinal and the wine was adequate, but it was free and there was plenty so it was good. The market was red-hot, it was time we started acting like it and having ourselves some good parties again. I wanted this one to blow everybody's mind, I wanted people to talk about this brokers' open for years.

I entered the house, fashionably late, like I was Mick Jagger finally showing up at a Stones' after-party. The place was swinging. Good job, Kirsten. Everybody knew me, everybody was grateful I'd finally arrived, wanted to shake my hand. Everybody wanted a piece of Rick, and who am I to deny them? Django Miller, from that new online outfit Zap Realty, handed me a glass of wine, Stag's Leap, decent stuff, not super expensive but good, good enough for these folks anyway. Zap was undercutting everybody, kicking 1.5% of sales costs back to the sellers. I wasn't sure what their angle was yet or how they planned on making a profit by selling dollars for 75 cents, but I guess that's how the Internet works.

Every realtor in Southern Marin was there. No way they'd miss a Rick Davies' open house. Not just for the free-flowing tipple and crudités and such—they knew that no matter what kind of house it was, whether it was a 5000-square-foot imitation Spanish hacienda on an acre with bay and city views going for $4 million, or a $600k shitbox in Birdland, I picked winners. That is, houses that sold quick, with minimal time and effort. We realtors hate houses that don't sell right away, ones you have to hang out in every other Sunday—or sometimes every Sunday if the owner is really anxious or a cretin—for months on end. Open houses are really a way for agents to find new customers, pass out business cards to the looky-loos. Serious buyers make the rounds with an agent on Saturday, the day *before* the opens.

"Thanks Django," I said, wondering why I had to thank him for serving me my own wine, and if I'd forgotten his name and called him "Django" by accident, because what the hell kind of moniker is Django anyway? Better than Shithead, I suppose. Didn't matter, I was the star and could do no wrong. I smiled, turned sideways and pushed through the crowd deeper into the bowels of the old house, past the addition (a sun room and fourth bedroom) and the converted garage. All unpermitted, of course, but nobody cared about that these days, especially if you were outside the town limits of Mill Valley proper and were subject to county inspections, which were a joke. Meanwhile, the president of San Francisco's Building Inspection Commission didn't bother to get a permit when he did a major overhaul of a spec house in the city. Nobody would have known if the damn thing hadn't collapsed and tumbled down a hill. I think he had to pay a $100 fine.

I worked the crowd like I owned the joint, which I sort of did. That is, I owned the exclusive-right-to-sell, for another 84 days, which was better than actually being on the hook for it. The "owner" couldn't sell it now without me. Well, they could still sell it themselves, to a neighbor or relative—but they'd still be on the hook for Charlie's broker's commission. All I had to do was find somebody to take this white elephant off our hands, and be quick about it, and I'd hit pay dirt. Without having to pay a mortgage, property taxes, water bills, electric bills, or gardeners. Even so, the quicker the better. See, that 6% commission buyers pay? Charlie would split it with the buyer's broker. Then I'd split it 50-50 with Charlie—my cut as salesperson is 1.5%. Do you think I'd rather sell your house in the first week for $900,000, or take four or five weeks of work to sell it for $1,000,000? That's a $100k difference for you, but not for me. See, I can make $13,500 in a week, or $15,000 in 3 months. Which do you think I prefer?

Besides, if a house doesn't sell right away, buyers start asking questions, like: "How old is the roof?" and "Does the furnace work?" and "Does the foundation need work?" Annoying shit like "Is this a flood zone?" and "Does it need a paint job?" and "Does it have insulation?" and "Did anybody ever die here?" and "Is it haunted?" Questions, questions, questions, and sooner or later you actually have to do a little research to answer them, instead of just sitting around and grinning, wearing your Sunday finery and talking about how this was the best neighborhood in town, the schools were great, you could get to the city in 15 minutes (OK, 15 minutes at 3:00 a.m., otherwise more like 45, but still). Me, when they start getting nosy, I like to say, "This house is gone in three days, you want it or not?"

So it's all about speed, not price. Meanwhile the suckers—I mean, my cherished clients—think I'm out to get them top dollar. They think I'm their friend. Why should I disillusion them? I just drop some self-help bureaucratic bullshit into the conversation, use the client's name a lot, look them right in the forehead so they know who's boss, then maybe drop down to the right eye to be friendly. Like Billy Dee Williams used to say about Colt 45, it works every time. Why people trust realtors, or used car salesmen, or politicians, it's all a great mystery. It's almost as if they *like* pulling the wool over their own eyes. Maybe it's the same thing as people watching movies: they know that Tom Cruise isn't really a superspy, it's all fake, and there's no way his character is going to go the way of all flesh, but they get nervous and excited anyway when he's "in danger." I suppose there must be some sort of genetic or evolutionary explanation for this. But that's above my pay grade. I don't know why the world is the way it is. It never fails to mystify, confound and sometimes astound me. I just accept my place in it, and use leverage accordingly.

Chapter 14

A white-coated waiter sauntered by and I grabbed two glasses of Mumm Napa sparkling wine off his tray. I threw down the first glass like President Bush at a wedding, putting my hip into it, quickly set the empty back on the waiter's tray before he made off and sipped at the second.

"Rick, how's it going?" asked Maggie Ashwill, one of Marin's most successful realtors. She was about five years younger than me, made three times as much money and was beautiful. In other words, I hated her, although I still wanted to get into her pants. But I was glad to see her show up—everything she touched turned to gold.

"Maggie, how are you?" I pecked her on the cheek.

"You know, same-same."

"I'm surprised to see you here—didn't think you worked the five-per-center slums."

"Why am I here? So I can hang around with you, stupid," she said, smiling mischievously and poking me in the chest.

"Who, me?" I asked, a little flustered by the physical contact. She knew I had a crush on her and liked to tease me.

"Yes, you. What, I wouldn't?"

I was about to make a witty rejoinder about a blizzard in Vacaville when I heard a commotion from out front.

"Where is he?" somebody shouted.

"Who? What do you want, how can I help you?" I heard Kirsten ask, all charm and professionalism.

"Rick Davies, we know he's here."

"Of course he's here, this is his brokers' open, and I don't appreciate you barging in like this. But I will get you a glass of wine if that will make you feel better," Kirsten said as I navigated through the crowd to see what all the fuss was about.

"Sorry ma'am, we're on duty…"

"Yes, of course, how about a fresh summer roll? Vegan or shrimp? Caviar, perhaps?" It wasn't Beluga sturgeon, of course, probably some farm-raised tilapia blend, but who knew the difference?

My pals Detectives Keyes and McGee were at the door. Kirsten was smart, hadn't invited them in. Cops, just like landlords, can't come in your house unless you invite them. Or they have a warrant. Or there are no witnesses.

"Hello officer, what's the problem?" I really wanted to say, "What the frack are you doing here, dickweeds?" But I was polite because I'd had experience with cops when I was younger and knew it was always better to be polite. I told you that story already, right? Sometimes I forget and repeat myself.

"Mr. Davies, I'd like you to come with us," said Detective Keyes. He looked like he hadn't slept in a couple of days; the coffee stains on his trenchcoat had multiplied, and his breath smelled like he'd been smoking even cheaper cigars, and more of them.

McGee stood next to Keyes, towering over him, quietly flexing his guns; the way his cheap suit bulged at the seams reminded me of those spicy Italian pork sausages they sell at the farmer's market. Behind them lurked Justin, black visor still down, like an Imperial Trooper from *Star Wars*. I supposed Keyes was the good cop and McGee the bad cop. I had Justin figured for the incompetent cop.

Enough was enough. "Excuse me, didn't we clear this up yesterday? This is bordering on harassment, I'm a citizen in this town, I pay taxes, I pay your salary, and I'm not going to…"

Of a sudden, I found myself face down on the fake Persian rug, involuntarily biting down hard as I could. Strangely, my immediate thought was how glad I was that the rug was brand new. I hate dust, and have an irrational fear of dust mites, even though almost everybody's eyelashes are infested with them already anyway. I felt like I'd just jumped into an ice bath. My limbs were rigid, catatonic.

"Don't tase him again bro!" Django shouted. I didn't know why everybody started laughing; I hadn't gotten into YouTube yet. I felt cuffs slapped on my wrists, gears grinding as they tightened them real tight. Have you ever been arrested? Been put in handcuffs? It's not the same as when your girlfriend does it, if you're into that sort of thing. The fuzz does it one of two ways. They can be nice about it, and leave them loose, in which case the cuffs are just an uncomfortable nuisance. Or they can be jabronis and ratchet the bracelets taut, bruising, maybe even breaking your wrists, so tight you lose circulation and it feels like your hands are going to fall off. They were clearly going with option two. Justin and McGee picked me up and half-carried, half-dragged me out to an unmarked Crown Vic and unceremoniously tossed me in the back seat like a sack of conventional potatoes. I heard the oohs and ahhs from the crowd of brokers, and maybe even a shriek or two. At least I was right about one thing: they'd be talking about this brokers' open for years. Everything went black.

Chapter 15

I felt my consciousness rising, gradually, then suddenly, rushing up like the rovers popping out of the ocean in the opening credits of *The Prisoner*, or the way Hemingway went bankrupt. Where was I? I mean, that's what I was thinking, I'm not coming back from a long digression. Or am I? Anyway, I was sore from head to foot, as if I'd been battered with a tire iron, fallen down a flight of stairs or had taken a Bikram yoga class. I was laying down on something hard and uncomfortable, a far cry from the Tempur-Pedic mattress I was accustomed to. I opened my eyes and found myself sprawled on a narrow wooden bench, covered with carved initials (the bench that is, not me—I skipped the whole tattoo fad). I sat up, groaned, and looked around. I was in a cell. It smelled like burnt rubber and urine, like a back alley, a parking garage, or London. I was glad to see I was the only one in lockup; sometimes it's better not to have company. I stood up shakily, and tottered over to the cell door. I grabbed the bars to steady myself and peered out. A morbidly obese guard, his best years behind him, if he ever had any, sat on a stool, massive glutes spilling over its edge, reading a copy of *People* magazine.

"Hello?"

He looked up at me and frowned. "Can't you see I'm reading, schmuck? Shut up and siddown."

I sat down. The bench was really hard. I noticed my suit was filthy, and torn at the knees and elbows. My once-beautiful Brunos were scuffed, and without laces. I remembered why I was here. Or at least how I got here. Sort of. I was mocus. I blinked my eyes a few times and half an hour went by. I started to feel both curious and bored, a very dangerous combination. Bored enough so that when the guard put down the *People*, I dared incurring his wrath again and asked, "Hey, you mind if I read that?" He frowned and tossed it at me.

I read every article in the magazine. I learned all about the spat between Jennifer Lopez and Marc Anthony (who was he, anyway?), Victoria Beckham's armpit cleavage, and Paris Hilton's latest photo shoot, in which she was captured for eternity, nude, in gold body paint. So much going on in the world that I'm unaware of. I really should go to jail more often, it opens up new horizons.

After I'd read every article, I read every ad. Then I went back and read every article and every ad all over again, to see if I'd missed anything good. I was so desperate for any diversion I figured I'd try to strike up a conversation. Maybe the guard was as bored as I was. He clearly didn't have much to do since I was his sole prisoner. Now he was reading a paperback of *Fire in the Hole*.

"Hey."

"What?" he demanded, glowering.

"You like that book?"

The guard closed the book over a finger. "Oh yeah, Elmore Leonard's the best. I love the character Raylan Givens from this story."

Elmore Leonard. Great way to bond with cops. Crooks, too. Dale Carnegie had nothing on me. "Me too, big Elmore fan. Haven't read that one yet. I'll pick it up. You like *Get Shorty*?"

"A classic. And even the sequel *Be Cool* was pretty good. The book that is, not the movie, the movie sucked."

"Yeah it did, didn't it? John Travolta phoned it in. Y'know it says in here"—I waved the *People* magazine—"that Travolta is gay. They even got a picture of him in here kissing a dude in front of his private plane."

"So?"

I shrugged. "Just making conversation."

"You're not very good at it."

The aroma of cheap cigars somehow cut through the funky jailhouse air. Detective Keyes strolled up, nodded at the guard. Keyes looked like he'd slept in his suit. Flying solo, no McGee. Fine by me. "I'll take it from here, Wally."

Wally, with great effort, stood up. I watched him struggle against gravity, fascinated; fatties are even rarer than conservatives, good restaurants and empathy in southern Marin. He waddled over and unlocked the cell door.

"Should I cuff him?"

Keyes chortled. "This fucking guy, you kidding?" He walked me down the corridor, holding me tight by the crook of my elbow.

"Hey, can I ask you something?"

"Sure."

"What am I in for?"

Keyes laughed as we entered a lime-green interogation room. It looked just like all the ones you've seen on cop shows, so I won't bother to describe it. We sat at opposite sides of a beat-up metal table.

"That's a first. Usually perps know exactly what they're here for, and talk my ear off about how they're innocent."

"But I am innocent!"

"How do you know? You don't even know why you're here!"

He had me there. Keyes was sharper than he looked. Or I wasn't. I changed the subject. "So who's the worst criminal you've ever had in here?" People love to talk about themselves, so I gave him a chance, show him I cared about him.

He sat up straight; I'd piqued his interest. He was, like most local LEOs, bored as hell and happy to spin a yarn for a literally captive audience. He leaned back in his chair, lacing his fingers behind his head, revealing big semicircular sweat stains under his arms. "What with how violent crime is such a rarity hereabouts, you'd think that the worst we'd get is B&E, skells busting into cars, that sort of crap. And we do get plenty of that, believe me. Despite the beautiful natural surroundings, the affluence, lotta folks are miserable, they're stressed as hell, and there's a bunch of them who use drugs. Sometimes they commit petty crimes to support their habits."

My eyes widened. "You don't say?" My regular routine—make the client think I'm interested in them, and listen attentively, forge a relationship—was working like a charm.

"I shit you not, friendo. Coupla times a year here we get some bad *hombres*, strung-out meth heads with guns, ripping off dealers. Even if half the time the dealers they target are juniors at Tam High who got in over their head, so it almost seems silly. But the guns are real."

"I guess sometimes the kids get more than they bargained for."

"Yup. You get some real bangers coming in from Marin City, Richmond or West Oakland, these over-privileged little punks don't know what hit 'em. Although every once in a while there's a local who's a real gangster. Like that kid who tried to shoot his ex-girlfriend and her new beau while they were sitting in a pickup truck, right on Evergreen, down the street from Whole Foods."

"Yeah, that was crazy, right? A drive-by shooting in Mill Valley!"

"And then it turned out the kid had stolen a Maserati from a famous chef and he drove it around for a year and they might never have caught him if he hadn't gotten fingered for the attempted murder!"

"Yeah, I read about that in the paper. He busted into the warehouse where the car was in storage, rappelled down from an open skylight like frickin' *Mission: Impossible*. Then he had a year-long joy ride, and nobody thought twice about it 'cause there's nothing suspicious about a 17-year-old with a Maserati in Mill Valley."

"Right? Maybe, if you play your cards right, you'll get to meet him once you get to the Q. But still, like I said, we don't get a lot of violent crime around here." He leaned forward over the table and lowered his voice."But when we do, it's bad. Real bad."

"Yeah? Like what?" I was intrigued. The worst crime I'd heard about since I'd moved to town was my neighbor complaining about somebody ripping off his *Sunday Times*. It got so bad the delivery guy started dropping off two copies, one for my neighbor, the other labeled "thief." You had to hand it to the thief, he had moxie, picking up a paper labeled "thief" every weekend. Then again, there was Marjorie Khan. And that other victim, the Yoga teacher.

"Well, recently we had a home invasion in Corte Madera. Some junkie broke into an old man's house and demanded cash, jewelry, whatever he thought the old-timer had."

"Oh yeah, I remember that. The old dude pretended he was really scared and asked the kid if he could use the toilet. Then he went into the bathroom and got his pistol, hidden behind the water tank, and came out blazing."

"Yup, like straight out of *The Godfather*. Turns out he was a WWII vet and could handle himself. Shot the kid three times. Showed him a thing or two."

"Yeah. But didn't the old man get shot in the face?"

Keyes shrugged. "You can't win 'em all. And of course, this being Marin, the kid's folks are now suing the old man for violating his civil rights. But that's nothing. Back in the '70s it was hella weird around here. Patty Hearst and the Symbionese Liberation Army, the Zebra Killers, Jim Jones, Harvey Milk, Presidential assassination attempts, the Zodiac. You heard of all that stuff, right?"

"Uh, yeah," I said, "Most of it." What the heck was a Zebra Killer?

"Things were seriously screwed up back then. You know that Milk and Moscone and the Reverend Jones were tight? They got Jones to send up busloads of his zombie followers from LA, they went around voting in every district, over and over again, using fake names. That's how Moscone won the election. Then him and Milk got shot—coincidentally—two weeks after Jonestown. Lotta people lost relatives down there. All of a sudden they're heroes. Nothing like a bullet to put you in a good light for posterity, you know what I'm saying?"

I did. I let him go on. This was way better than *People*.

"Then there Marin's very own psycho, the Trailside Killer. You ever hear about him?"

"Don't think so. When was that?"

"Like I was saying, numbnuts, the '70s. So much crazy shit went down, people forget about the Trailside Killer. I dunno, maybe 'cause they never made a movie about him. Here's the deal: a woman was shot point blank in the back of the head while hiking on Mt. Tam. There were some suspects, but nothing came of it, they just wrote it off as another one of those awful '70s things. Then the next spring another lady was murdered while hiking on a different, nearby trail, this time stabbed."

"Jesus, but those trails are so crowded, how come nobody saw anything?"

"That's just it, somebody *did* see something. Another hiker saw her get shivved."

"So they caught the killer?"

"Nope. And you know why? Because the eyewitness description was completely wrong."

"Huh?"

"Happens all the time. The brain is not only a terrible thing to waste, ya know, it's just plain terrible. You ever been to traffic school?"

"Who me? I seem like the kinda guy who gets in trouble?" I said from my hard metal chair inside the depressing room. I shifted my weight. My ass was starting to hurt. I preferred the leather-wrapped Italian foam of my Eames chair. I remembered Jason the motorcycle cop's recommendation, and made a mental note to sign up for traffic school when—if—I got sprung.

Keyes laughed, his eyes dead. "You're funny, I like you."

I didn't believe him. Where was all this leading, anyhow? Did he really want to interrogate me, or was this just an excuse for him to shoot the breeze?

"OK. They show you this video of a bunch of mooks passing a basketball back and forth, and they tell you, 'count how many times the ball is passed' and this goes on for two minutes or so. When it's over they ask you, 'how many times did they pass the ball?' and you say, 'sixteen' or 'fourteen' or whatever, and then they ask, 'OK, did you see the gorilla?' and you're like 'huh?'"

"Gorilla?"

"Yeah, halfway through the movie a guy in a fuckin' gorilla suit walks across the floor. And it's not like he's hurrying or anything, he even stops and waves right at the camera. But nine out of ten people don't see him. You know why?"

"Beats me."

I could tell he was pleased to tell me why. "They call it normalcy bias." He stopped and stroked his chin. "Or maybe it's cognitive dissonance. Whatever. You're watching for one thing, and then something else completely out of context appears before your eyes, and your mind refuses to process the information. It acts like a computer getting a bad data entry and just tosses it away, so the information never reaches your consciousness."

"Wow."

"Indeed. You see something that you think can't possibly be happening on your local bucolic hiking trail, like some dame getting stabbed in the freakin' neck, you're watching it but your brain refuses to process it, so you fill in the details later with whatever similar memories are floating around your mind. A lot of times it's scenes from a movie or TV show and you get it confused with real life."

"Like Ronald Reagan."

"Bingo. That's why eyeball witnesses are so unreliable."

"That's wild. But if you don't mind me saying so, you seem unusually, uh, erudite for a cop."

"I'm not career police. I took this gig to make ends meet while I get my real business off the ground. I'm a software entrepreneur."

Chapter 16

"Uh, OK, sure." Of course, of course he was. There are a lot of delusional folks in California, and Californians think Marinites are delusional. This joker probably built an Angelfire web site in 1995, replete with flaming GIFs, a scrolling title bar and blink tags, and thought he was the next Bill Gates. Just like every waiter in Hollywood has a spec script in his back pocket, every jamoke in the Bay Area who ever learned basic HTML has a an idea for The Next Big Thing. I had a big idea too, I think I told you. That's what got me into hot water in the first place. Or was it? I can't remember.

"'Uh, OK, sure,'" Keyes repeated in a high-pitched whine, mocking me. "Yeah I know you, you think I'm some piece of shit who used to boost 8-tracks from cars when I was in high school, had a choice of becoming a cop, a guard or an inmate, am I right?"

"I never said…"

"Check this out, shitbird." Keyes pulled a large black doohickey from his shirt pocket. "Know what this is?"

It looked to be the same contraption Barney had shown me the other day. "It's one of those e-Phones, right?"

"iPhone, lamebrain. And there's a new model coming out next month. My sister-in-law? Her cousin's kid babysits for Guy Kawasaki's dentist. Guy says the next generation will support something called apps."

"Apps?"

"Yeah, they're like little programs that perform discrete tasks. It's gonna be huge. And I have a great idea. When you're watching TV, and the sound is muddled, if somebody in the room says 'What'd he say?' the DVR winds back ten seconds and closed captions are…"

The landline phone attached to the wall rang, interrupting his sales pitch. Keyes picked it up. "Keyes." He cast a sideways glance at me. "Yeah. Really? You sure?" He hung up the phone, looked at me and scowled. "Let's go."

I guess he was mad he couldn't finish his dog-and-pony show, as if the ending wasn't obvious enough. Who knew, maybe it was all bullshit. Who the hell is Guy Kamasutra anyway? Lots of people out here have good raps, telling you how they used to ride on Ken Kesey's bus, or ran with the Panthers back in the day, or that they were childhood friends with Steve Jobs. Sometimes you just didn't know who, or what, to believe. But you never wanted to dismiss anybody out of hand; anything is possible in California.

Keyes opened the interrogation room door and led me down the spotless hallway. We took an elevator up to the main floor, light filtering in through the overhead skylights, just like Frank Lloyd Wright intended. We turned a corner and there was Kirsten. Waiting for me. Dressed to the nines. A smoking hot tomato.

"He's all yours." Keyes handed me a manilla envelope with my Treo and wallet inside. Good thing I wasn't holding when they tased me.

"Thanks, officer." Kirsten and Keyes exchanged a look; I guess she was letting him know how mad she was at him for ruining the brokers' open. She turned to me. I was glad to see her but didn't let her know it. She looked me over, head to toe. "You're different, somehow—hardened."

"Six hours inside will do that to a man."

"My goodness, I hope you didn't get turned out."

"You know what they say—do the time, don't let the time do you. But a man has needs. I held out for 45 minutes before I let somebody make me their bitch."

"Impressive will power. I admire your, ah, rectitude."

"That's what he said."

"C'mon, let's get out of here."

"You know that line is in like every movie ever made?"

"He's right," said Keyes with a friendly wave. "And Mr. Davies, if you want, I could drop off a deck at your office."

"A what?"

"You know, a PowerPoint presentation for my app. In case you know any angel investors."

"Oh sure, of course, looking forward to it, you take care now!" What is it somebody once said? Power corrupts, PowerPoint corrupts absolutely.

"Check it out before you come back. Once you've been here once, you guys always come back."

Kirsten took my arm and we strolled down the well-lit corridor. "Aw, you've made a friend."

"I can't help the way God made me, can I? I'm like freshly baked bread—everybody loves me. That's what my mom says anyways."

She kept mum. I liked that. I thought for a second we were going to do Dashiell Hammett dialogue all day. It was fun for a minute but it made me tired to imagine extending this badinage much further.

We stepped outside into hot brittle air. The sun was bright and without shade. The asphalt parking lot warmed my feet through what used to be my best shoes. There weren't any laces in the manilla envelope, and the Maglis kept slipping off. Marin's climate is strange—it always feels hot when the sun is shining, no matter the temperature. But if you're in the shade, you cool off right away. And no matter how hot it is during the day, it gets cold at night, as if you were in the desert, or high in the mountains. But it's not a desert, there's lush greenery everywhere, and those redwood trees didn't get that big from lack of water. High in the mountains? Nah, we're at sea level. So why does the air feel so thin? I could tell you but I don't know. Maybe I'll look it up one of these days.

Kirsten had a brand-new silver BMW M6 convertible, the sports package model. Heated leather seats, 12-speaker surround sound, 20-inch wheels. Nice. The one I really wanted but had to settle for a 3 series—Basic Marin Wheels. She slid behind the wheel and put on a pair of giant white sunglasses, just like Paris Hilton was wearing in the article I'd just been reading.

"Sweet ride."

"Thanks." She inspected me, then crinkled her nose. "You need a new suit. And a shower."

"Yeah." My beautiful Brioni was torn and filthy. "I can't wait to burn this monkey suit. Say, what happened to the Hummer?"

"Didn't seem like the right sled for a gun moll to pick up a notorious criminal from the hoosegow—didn't wanna draw the heat." She pressed the play button on the CD player and weird music blared all around me. It sounded like somebody put Public Enemy and Bob Marley in a blender, with a girl rapping in a foreign language layered on top. I kind of liked it, but didn't want to ask what it was because I didn't want to seem unhip, so I can't tell you what it was.

"We heading back to the office?"

"Nope."

"Don't I need to straighten out bail money, figure out how much I owe Charlie?"

She kept her eyes on the road. "Bail you out? Charlie fired your sorry ass."

Chapter 17

Fired? Me? I sold over $12 million last year! OK, it was only six houses, but still. I watched the wind blow wisps of blonde hair around Kirsten's head, like she was a film star in a perfume commercial. Me, I was beat, a mess, humiliated. I hurt all over. Yet I couldn't help but check her out. I combed my disarrayed mop with my fingers, a half-assed attempt at making myself presentable. She glanced over, caught my eyeballing and gave me a half smile, but I couldn't read her expression behind her mammoth sunglasses.

"Cat got your tongue?"

We rolled south on the 101. I looked straight ahead, stunned. Mount Tam was wrapped in fog. It was like the mountain was floating up to the sky and disappearing in mist. I waited till I felt like I could speak without sputtering. "But…I make it rain! I'm a top-performing agent!"

"You mean you *were*. Sometimes though, people's perceptions are more important than money."

I laughed out loud. "In this business? Are you kidding? What's more important than the shekels?"

"In realty? Reality. Like, perception is reality, you know what I'm saying? Didn't you ever read the Bhagavad Gita? Or Ekhart Tolle? Long term, a bad reputation means no more money. Like, who wants to be known as the employer of a murderer?"

"Murder? What? Is that why the cops hauled me in? Then why'd they let me go?"

She rambled on, ignoring me. "I mean, if you put your house up for sale, would you want Squeaky Fromme laying down her rap at an open house on Sunday? Even if she wore a nice pantsuit, people get put off by the swastika carved in the forehead, right?"

Kirsten was funny and mean at the same time. I couldn't tell if she was doing it intentionally or if it was just how she was. I liked it. I took a closer look at her, in the sunshine and the wind. She looked pretty good. She was on the wrong side of 40 but could pass for 27 if you squinted.

I shrugged. "I dunno. Maybe you'd want a murderer-agent if the house was notorious, like if you were selling John Wayne Gacy's place, you could be all like, 'Speaking as a killer myself, I was impressed by the deep sump-pump pits in the basement. You could hide a body in there for weeks if you had to, before you could properly dispose of it!'"

She laughed and gave me another quick turn and a smile. She reminded me of Sharon Stone in *Basic Instinct*. It occurred to me that was kind of a creepy joke for her to laugh at. What if she's a total whack job like Sharon Stone? I mean a whack job like her character in *Basic Instinct*, not the regular real-life whack job Sharon Stone. I realized I didn't know this dame from Adam, or Eve, whatever, or even where she was taking me. What if we were headed to her beachfront mansion at Stinson Beach right now? I remembered seeing *Basic Instinct* on basic cable a couple of years after I moved to California. Of course I didn't know any better before—and apparently the producers knew most people wouldn't either—but I cracked up when they said Sharon's character lived at Seadrift, which is a small, gated community right on the beach at Stinson, a very flat area, but when you got to Sharon Stone's house on Seadrift in the movie, it was high up in the cliffs of…where? Big Sur? I guessed the filmmakers figured, ah, what the hell, only ten million people will know the difference, who cares? It looks better this way. But then why did they use the name of a real part of Stinson Beach, to make it worse? I'm thinking that the guy who wrote the screenplay (who lived in Tiburon, by the way) used that old trick of using real place names to make it seem like he knew what he was talking about, and then the director went ahead and did whatever he wanted, without regard for what we called in English 101 verisimilitude.

Anyway, Kirsten had my head up my ass, and not for the last time. I was the suspected murderer here, so why was I scared of her? "Um, so you'll excuse me for axing you, but um, why are you hanging around with an alleged killer? Aren't you afraid of me? And, by the way, who the hell am I supposed to have murdered anyhow?"

She tried to furrow her brow and managed a slight frown. "Seriously? You don't know?"

"All I know is that I've been beat up, I'm sore all over, tired, hungover and could really use a drink. What say we pop over to the Deuce?"

"Your friend Barney."

I didn't trust her, not as far as I could throw her, so I played dumb. I found it easy. "Huh? I heard Barney died yesterday but what do I have to do with it?"

"You heard he had a weak heart?"

"I heard he died of a heart attack."

"Bum ticker. He was only in his fifties, but he'd had heart attacks before, and half a dozen stents. And you know what's really bad for a weak heart?"

"Exercise?"

"Cocaine."

"Oh shit."

"Yeah. Your fingerprints were all over the vial they found on Barney's shag rug. And one of the guys on his crew saw you hand Barney the blow. Apparently he was blasting Edgar Winter's "Frankenstein" on his vintage Pioneer when he bit it. The record was skipping when they found him, draped over an old dresser. That's why the cops investigated—his neighbor was going crazy from hearing that riff over and over."

I could hardly blame the neighbors for being annoyed by the riff that made punk rock necessary. "It's not my fault, I had no idea, I thought…"

"Sure, you thought you were being a pal. Everybody likes blow, right? And it's harmless and non-addictive, right? Dude, the '80s have been over for a long time now."

I stared straight ahead. For the second time in a few minutes, she'd rendered me mute.

"But you know what's even worse for you than cocaine?"

I shrugged. When I was younger I thought there was nothing better for you, so I was stumped.

"Arsenic. I've never heard of anybody snorting it before, but that's gotta smart. Probably worse than the blow washed with gasoline we used to do back in the day. You'd get a nosebleed after the third line, but that didn't stop you, once you got started."

She called it "blow," just like Senator Obama did in his autobiography. That's what heavy users, not casual weekend dabblers, called it. At least the heavy users I used to know. Like me.

"Arsenic? That's crazy?"

"Right? I know! Crazier than huffing gasoline-laced coke even."

"Why do they think there's arsenic in it?"

"That's the working theory. They're still analyzing what was left over in the vial, it won't be done till Monday, that was the CSI guy's guess. See, the cops figured it was a heart attack from the coke, but the CSI guy noticed Barney's fingernails were discolored—that's a classic sign of arsenic poisoning."

"Jesus." I paused. "So…why did you get me out of jail? What makes you think I didn't do it?"

"I never said I didn't."

Chapter 18

She suspected I was a killer, but didn't seem too concerned. I found this deeply disturbing. But also deeply exciting. She exited the highway onto Tiburon Boulevard. We went over a bump and I realized I had a giant woody.

"Pfft, you're no killer."

I was glad she thought I was innocent, but she somehow managed to make it sound insulting at the same time, like I wasn't manly enough to murder. I stared straight ahead, cool air gusting through my hair. It felt good.

"You mind telling me where we're going?"

"My place in Tiburon. There might be reporters at your house, and you never know, the cops might change their minds and haul you in again. It'll take 'em a little longer to find you out here."

"How do you know I'm innocent?"

"Innocent? That's a good one. I didn't say I thought you were innocent—I just don't think you're a killer."

"Why not?" I tried not to sound miffed.

"Listen Rick, let me be up front with you, OK? I've been around the block, not once, like a dozen times. Known my fair share of, uh, unsavory dudes. Besides, I asked around about you, people say you're unreliable, irresponsible and two-faced, but you're also kind of a wuss, so I just can't feature it."

"I'm very reliable!" Of a sudden, I remembered where I got the coke from. "Holy smokes, I think we should go back and talk to the cops. I just realized something."

"What?"

"The blow I gave to Barney, I got it from a client, who, uh, gave it to me. We gotta go back to the cops and tell 'em it wasn't mine!"

"Great idea, head back to the fuzz, and tell them that you gave Barney poison coke, but you didn't know it was poison, and you might know where it came from. As your attorney, I strongly advise you to clam up."

"But I want to…"

"You know what cops and realtors have in common?"

There she goes again, throwing me another curveball. "What's that?"

"They both love quick sales."

"Whaddya mean?"

"You know exactly what I mean. You walk into the police station talking shit like that, maybe they're not sure you did it, but they sure as hell don't like *you*. They don't know if you're their guy or not, but they're 100% sure you're a sleazeball, so they're happy to put you away for it. Maybe you're not the right sleazeball for this particular case, but what do they care? You're a sleazeball nonetheless, and if you didn't do this, they figure you did something else, or you'll do something else eventually, so they're happy to hang it on you. They'll get the real perp another day—meanwhile, case closed, mark it green on the board, have a doughnut and relax."

"How do you know so much about police work?"

"I watch a lot of cop shows on TV. Good ones, like *Homicide*. I've also read a lot of Elmore Leonard books."

"Really? Me too! So does the guard back at the…" I trailed off as she stared at me, stone-faced. "OK, you know I'm not a murderer, but why are you protecting me?"

"Protecting you? Slow down there, cowboy. Lemme tell you something." We were at the traffic light just after the 101 overpass. She turned around and pointed up over my shoulder at the fog-laced mountain overlooking the highway. "Oh wow, lookit Mount Tam, so beautiful. Have you ever been up there on a clear day? You can see like 40 miles in every direction, it's amazing." The light turned and she took a left towards Tiburon.

What was up with her? ADD? Or maybe just stoned? "Nah, not yet, one of these days."

"Heh. I know your type. New Yorker, you miss real bagels and a good slice. Probably came out for a visit in October and decided to move here, not knowing how shitty it gets in the winter rainy season, or the summer foggy season. But still it's better than the east coast, right? It's like folks in San Rafael say, the weather in Mill Valley is terrible…"

"Yadda yadda yadda, East Coast, etc."

"Right. And when you lived in New York you never went to the Statue of Liberty and now you have no interest in going to the top of Mt. Tam, seeing it from down here is close enough."

"You've got me pegged." She was starting to really get my goat, which somehow made me want to knock boots with her even more.

"Damn straight I do. Anyway, let me tell you something. When I was younger I ran with a rough crowd."

"You mean like you dropped acid and went to Dead shows?"

She kept her eyes on the road as we rolled by Blackie's Pasture. "Well yeah, sure, everybody did that, but I meant more like I hung out with bikers and did meth. Real, like, motherfuckers, you know what I'm saying?"

"I think so." I'd known some myself. Had a friend on East 3rd Street who used to sell pot to the Angels, when their clubhouse was across the street. Fun people to hang out with, until you inevitably pissed them off for some reason and they beat you to a pulp. We both fell silent for a moment, but it wasn't an awkward silence, more like a comfortable pause, and I realized she was opening up to me, but I didn't understand why. Maybe she didn't either. "Isn't this a little personal? We barely even know each other."

"That's what I'm trying to get past, not knowing each other. I'm just being up front with my feelings. I know some pretty tawdry shit about you already, so what have I got to lose? It's not like we work together anymore."

We turned left off the main drag and headed up the hill. "Oh yeah." I'd forgotten already that my good friend Charlie had shit-canned me. I'm sure she didn't want to, but I understood why she had to. Still, I wished she'd told me herself, face-to-face. What kind of asshole boss lets a subordinate do their firing for them? I wasn't worried about making a living; frankly, I needed some time off. I could find another gig when I needed it—there was always work for rainmakers like me. Maybe I'd call that jackal Django and see if he could get me into his Internet cyber online outfit. They were brand-new, and hopefully weren't too particular about their employees' personal lives. Silicon Valley, fog a mirror and you're in, right? In the meantime, maybe I could finally complete my sci-fi masterpiece.

"What I'm getting at, killers, they got a special...vibe about 'em, you know what I mean?"

"That thousand-yard stare?"

"What, you been watching war movies? Nah, it's more like an aura. Once you've met a murderer, you can spot one a mile away."

"I'm not a killer? That's a relief."

She laughed. We pulled to a stop in front of an ornate, wrought-iron gate barring the road. I didn't notice it till then but for a little while now we'd actually been on a private road. She pushed a clicker clipped to her sun visor and the gate hummed and slid open. "It is, isn't it? Hey, do you mind if I smoke?"

"Are you kidding? I'd love it if you smoke, especially if you gave me one."

"They're in my bag." She indicated the jump seat with a flick of her head.

I reached back into her black leather bag. I don't know jack about handbags but I know leather; Kirsten's was soft, smooth and supple to the touch, obviously expensive. I dug around and fished out a pack of American Spirits and a gold-plated Zippo. I took out two, lit them both and handed one to her. I hadn't smoked in years but it seemed like a great time to start up again. Our fingers brushed together and an electric shock went up my arm. She gave me some side-eye as we drove up the long private driveway.

Chapter 19

I took a deep, drawn-out drag on the butt and blew out a big blue nimbus. Like I said, I hadn't had a cigarette in ages; they were less socially acceptable than marijuana, non-grass-fed meat or child discipline in Southern Marin. The first cig, in the car driving up to her house, man, that felt good. This one, the second one, was even better.

"I've been meaning to ask…if I got fired, why did you bail me out?"

"Really? That's what you want to talk about? After what I just showed you?"

I smiled. "Yeah, I liked that." I turned on my side and put an arm on the small of her back. She shifted, pushing my hand away.

"Hey, what's that all about? I figured you liked me now."

"Who said I liked you? I just needed a good boning."

I appreciated her honesty if not the sentiment. I quickly returned to my default state of confusion. "You bailed me out 'cause you were horny?"

She lowered her forehead into her palm. "Jesus, you're a goddamn moron, you know that?" She got up off the bed. I took a good look; everything had happened so fast I hadn't had a chance till now. Her tummy was a little poochy, and there was cellulite on her heinie and thighs. But the overall concept was sound and I approved. "I'll be right back, fool. By the way, your suit is disgusting. I'm gonna toss it." She picked the Brioni off the floor where she'd thrown it after so recently ripping it off me.

"But what will I wear?"

"Don't worry, I got you covered." She went into the bathroom, carrying the suit, and shut the door. I heard water running.

I sat upright in her bed while I waited for her to complete her ablutions. She was taking her sweet time. What else is new? The bed was super comfortable. I didn't know what kind of bed it was, but it was even more cozy than my Tempur-pedic. I felt underneath the mattress till I found a tag. Hästens. Fifty grand, easy.

I gazed out the bedroom's wall of windows. The view was sensational: Richardson Bay, the city softly glowing beyond it, and, as Kirsten came back into the room, it was framed by the soft curve of her shapely alabaster butt, its hue in sharp contrast to the rest of her permanently tanned skin. A view that would easily add half a million smackers to the value of this place. The skyline, I mean. The ass is sold separately. She sat on the bed and lit another pair of cigarettes and handed one to me. My first wasn't done yet, so I put it out and accepted the fresh replacement.

"OK, you got me. If you just started working for Charles le Chauve, where'd you get the bail dough? It must have been a pretty penny." Not to mention, how could she afford to live in a palace like this?

"I said I really needed a *job*, I didn't say I was *broke*. And I never even said..."

"Sure but..."

"Y'know, *really needing a job* is not the same thing as *really needing the money*. You'd think a big real estate tycoon like you would know that."

I was starting to catch on, but for some reason of reverse pride didn't want her to know that. "Whaddya mean?"

She sucked her cigarette, clutching the sheet to her chest so I couldn't see her titties, the way they do in PG-13 movies. Like I said, she was still quite fine but no spring chicken, so her boobs were a little droopy, and she seemed embarrassed about them. Or maybe she'd had kids and her nips were all messed up. I didn't care. I'm not that shallow. And it's not like I'm in mint condition myself. Maybe now that I was unempl...er, freelancing, I'd start hitting the gym again. Maybe.

"It's way complicated. I have capital, but it's all tied up. I want to buy this house and I need a mortgage."

"Which house?"

She rolled her eyes. "*This* house, the one we're in now, dummy."

Not for the first or last time, she caused my bafflement to deepen. "This isn't your house?"

She stared at me like she was regretting having brought me here more and more with each passing second. "That's what I just said, right?" She took a hard pull and blew smoke at me. "It's a long story, I'll spare you the gory details. This is my parents' house. As you can see, they did well for themselves. Worked hard, saved, invested, the whole '70s Republican success trip. Dad was in a business where he could make a lot of money, quickly, if he was smart about it and was willing to, um, take some ethical liberties."

"Realtor?"

She laughed, a rough *haw haw haw*, just like Hunter S. Thompson said the Hell's Angels do. "No, not all scumbags are in real estate. My pop, his bag was criminal law. Maybe you heard of him?" She told me his name and I whistled, long and low.

"I didn't realize I was hob-nobbing with aristocracy."

"Hob-nobbing? Is that what you call what we just did?" She smirked at me coquettishly and I smiled back. Then she tried to frown but couldn't quite manage it. I think that was the instant I realized she was nuts. Deep in the recesses of my mind, a warning bell started clanging. I should have dashed out the door toot sweet, but I was already snared in a honey trap, even if I didn't know it yet. I could have saved myself an awful lot of trouble if I'd just split then and there. But then I wouldn't be telling you this story, and I suppose your entertainment trumps my misery, so there you go. Besides, we'd just had a helluva romp, which, I've found, goes hand in hand with crazy, and I was hoping for another round as soon as we caught our breath.

"But c'mon, aristocracy, man? My dad was from Jersey, and he could only afford this house if he worked all the time. He was never here. Thank

God. He spent most of his time at Your Black Muslim Bakery and hanging with the Weathermen and the SLA and whatever else drug dealers used to call themselves."

"Where are your folks now? They're not gonna suddenly burst in and find I've deflowered their daughter?"

"I sure hope not. That would be hella weird since they're both dead."

Stepped in it again. "I'm sorry, I…hadn't heard."

"Yeah. Here, gimme that ashtray." She stubbed out her butt, shook another loose from the pack and sparked it. "Last year. Small plane crash. Dad was taking Mom to Cabo in the Piper Cub. Ironing out some wrinkles for Sammy Hagar's new club. They never made it."

"Oh wow, yeah, I *did* hear about that, I didn't put two and two together. Jesus, I'm sorry."

"Don't be. They were both total dicks."

"Whoa, that's kinda harsh. I mean, aren't everybody's parents? Then maybe you get a little older and you realize you're just like them?" I didn't know why I was arguing with her; my dad was a piece of work too.

"No," she said sternly. "Dude, I'm nothing like them. They were full-on heavy-duty assholes."

"At least they left you something. My dad bit it three months ago. All I got was a bottle of morphine pills, and I had to steal those from hospice. Comes in handy for hangovers, but I wasn't happy to find out he'd done a reverse mortgage on his house without telling me. What a scam those are, the way they…"

"My folks died intestate."

"They died on the interstate? Wait I thought you said they were flying down to Cabo, not driving."

She stared at me. I could tell she thought I was a dolt, but really I'm just hard of hearing. I have tinnitus from that time in '88, I was on shrooms and put my head in the speaker for an entire Red Rocks show. Come to think of it, maybe I am a dolt. As long as we both agreed on that, it worked to my advantage.

"Like, they didn't have a will? You know, the cobbler's kid not having shoes. The state is processing the estate and taking their sweet time. We're fighting the escheat in probate court." I remembered something about that from the Real Estate Principles course I took at Marin Community College a bunch of years ago when I first got my salesperson's license, but I forget what it means.

"I've got a bundle coming to me, but my cash flow sucks and I need to buy this place soon or else I'm gonna lose it. Like I said, it's complicated, irrevocable trusts and Swiss bank accounts and interlocking corporations in the Cayman Islands, the kinda setups I can't make heads or tails of. There's tons of cash in the bank, but I can't touch it for a year at least, and I've got a shitty credit rating from when I was…irresponsible in the '90s. So I gotta take a damn job so I can show income and get a mortgage. Can you believe that hassle?"

I'd heard this rich kid boho boo-hoo blather before. I tried to think of a diplomatic way to broach the subject of handling the sale of this house, if she couldn't get a mortgage. It would be a helluva commission.

"You can't get a NINJA loan? You know, stated income?"

"My bad credit has bad credit."

It must have been really, really bad. I'd recently sold a house in Petaluma to a guy from El Salvador, a nice 3-2 for $800,000. He used a stated income loan and claimed he made $150,000 a year playing in a mariachi band. His only proof: a Polaroid picture of himself wearing a mariachi costume. Approved! He put down 0% and got one of those 110% interest-only loans they were handing out back then to every Tom, Dick and José, so he got the house with no money down and walked out of the office with eighty grand in cash. He'd be fine as long as the mariachi biz stayed red hot.

"I hope you work something out. There's never been a better time to buy."

"Yeah, me too. You hungry?"

Chapter 20

Kirsten skedaddled out of bed, but before I could settle back and enjoy the show, she'd slipped on a fluffy white terry-cloth bathrobe, the kind Tony Soprano used to wear when he went out to get his newspaper.

"What about me? Got an extra robe?"

She blanched. I could see that somehow the idea sickened her. Like she was OK with us inserting various bodily parts inside each other, but not me wearing one of her bathrobes. Weirdo.

"I've got some clothes for you. We got rid of most of Dad's when he died, but I kept some for sentimental reasons. They should fit, he was about your size. Or at least he was after he went to seed."

She entered a walk-in closet which was bigger than my living room. I heard her rustling around. She returned bearing a pile of neatly folded duds and handed them to me, smirking. Mickey Mouse boxers, argyle socks, a turquoise Ban-Lon shirt and a white safari leisure suit. Casual rich lawyer garb, '70s style. I put them on—what choice did I have?—while she watched, giggling.

I followed her out to the great room and sat down at a Reef dining table while Kirsten opened a built-in Sub-Zero fridge big enough to hide a linebacker in. The view here was even better than the bedroom (except we were dressed now and I couldn't see her rear end anymore). One whole side of the house was glass, floor to ceiling, affording a priceless vista of Sausalito, Tiburon, the Golden Gate Bridge and the city. OK, not priceless—we have formulas for this sort of thing, and everything has a price. But pricey.

Me, I've seen plenty of priceless views before—they're a dime a dozen in Tiburon. Or a dime a half million? Anyway, the furniture—that was a different matter. Have I told you I'm into furniture? I'm proud of my

Eames lounger, but this roost was tricked out like a mid-century modern museum—sofas by Mies van der Rohe, Wegner wing chairs, vintage egg chairs, a chaise lounge by Le Corbusier. And the artwork: Tomasselli pill paintings, Hirst diamond-encrusted skulls, giant Mapplethorpe photographs of guys biting whips, a couple of Warhol soup cans. I don't know much about art but I do read the *New York Times* style section, so I recognized it and knew it cost serious swag. There was a whole lot more I couldn't place, older-looking stuff, pictures of fruit baskets and sunsets and ballerinas and what not, second-tier Impressionists, Gaugin's nephew or cousin, that were still probably worth millions, considering what a genuine Gaugin will run you these days. Then again, these digs were so ritzy, they might have been the real McCoy.

"I'll make us dinner."

"Awesome." I was starving, hadn't eaten all day, and there's nothing like a good game of hide-the-salami to work up an appetite.

"You like Cobb salad?"

"Sure," I lied, going with the flow. I would have preferred a big juicy steak, but at least a Cobb salad had bacon in it, if memory served. Turned out, no surprise, she's a health nut, so instead of bacon there was some kind of weird substitute called, maybe because it made you feel like you were in hell, "seitan." Instead of chicken breast, tofu. Even the eggs were fake. To add insult to injury, she used kale instead of iceberg lettuce. I picked at the fake-on or whatever the heck you call it.

"Here," she said, "have a gluten-free roll." This was the first I'd heard of glutens. I took a bite of the so-called roll, slathered in some kind of butter substitute. It tasted like a piece of old cardboard a homeless person had used to wipe his ass. Kirsten gave me the low down on healthy living while I picked at the dreadful salad. Not just about glutens—she hipped me to the problem with vaccinations, why I should meditate at least 15 minutes a day, the power of prayer, and *A Course In Miracles*. She was like a New Age Elmer Gantry.

"...and even worse are the frankenfoods they're shoving down our throats. Who knows what that junk does to you after you eat it for a few years? Scares the hell out of me."

I was getting scared too, all right, but not of GMOs, whatever the hell those were—I thought a GMO was a kind of Pontiac. I still couldn't figure out why I was here and what we were doing together. I started thinking about that Stephen King movie with Kathy Bates. None of this made any sense. Not the way I got out of jail, how she picked me up, what happened to Barney, why I was here now, the connection between fluoridated water and autism, none of it.

"Fine. I'll cut down on the bagels. They're no good out here anyway. But what I really wanna know is, what's your part in all this? Why do you care about me?"

"Who said I give a damn about you?" She sat down at the table and sipped her herbal tea. "I'm in it for the entertainment value. I'm freakin' bored out of my skull! I want some excitement out of life. Guys like you, you've got a bajillion deals going, you're running around all day, partying all the time, never a spare minute. You have no idea what it's like for us older, single women. This county is boris. Sleepy-time snoozesville. There's nothing to do here if you don't get loaded." She put a hand on my shoulder and looked me directly in the right eye, the same way I do when I'm closing. "I need to find meaning in my life. I want to help you find the real killer."

Chapter 21

"You mean like OJ? When he was looking for his wife's killer on all those golf courses."

"OJ didn't do it."

Of course not. "Huh?" What next? Was she going to show me her collection of serial killer trading cards?

"It was his son, the kid was a violent sociopath, he was on antidepressants, and his parents didn't know anything about non-violent communication, and who knows how many vaccinations he had growing up? OJ covered for him. Cops never went after the kid because they were all about OJ. You know how cops are, they're like bulldogs—once they have a suspect in mind, they won't let him go."

"Yes, so you've said."

"Rilly. What were we talking about again?

"About how you think I'm not the real killer."

"Riiiiight. Let's start at the beginning. You say a client gave you the blow."

"Yeah. I mean, sort of. You my lawyer now?"

"No, I'm not licensed. But I used to eavesdrop on my dad while he yacked on the phone, and he would take me with him to the courthouse when Mom was too hungover or depressed to get out of bed. But I'm better than a real lawyer, 'cause a real lawyer will tell you not to tell them anything they don't want to know, and I want you to tell me everything." She leaned forward, smiling in that upside-down way, making a platform with her hands and resting her chin on it.

"There's not much to tell. At the old lady's house—Mrs.

Papadopoulos—the house where, you know, we were having the brokers' open…"

"Yes, I remember. It was like eight hours ago. I was there."

I ignored her snark. It was hard to believe it really was just this morning. "Two days ago, she asked me to check out her attic, to see if there was anything up there that was worth anything, you know, before we cleaned out the place."

"She trusted you."

"Yeah."

"She's not as smart as I thought. Go ahead."

Or maybe she's smarter than both of us. "She had some nice old furniture up there, nothing too special, but you know, well-made 100-year-old stuff."

"I'm sure you told her you'd be happy to take it off her hands."

"Of course. And yes I dug through the drawers, you never know what you'll find in there. I hope I'm not shocking you."

"Shocking. Fer sure."

"So I'm poking around, and I come across a box filled with paraphernalia."

"'Paraphernalia?' Who are you, Joe Friday?"

"Not just your basic Marin cocaine grinder, straws and razor blades. Serious stuff—syringes, a bent spoon. Somebody was into some heavy shit. And, yeah, a vial of white powder." I didn't mention the cash, Krugerrands and acid at this juncture; there are some things you shouldn't even tell your lawyer.

"Aha."

"Obviously the old lady had no idea what was there, otherwise she wouldn't have asked me to look, right? I don't know who the drug gear belonged to—her sister's husband who croaked 20 years ago, or maybe she's got some derelict relative. Whatever, I thought I'd spare her the heartache and just toss the stuff. Ignorance is bliss and all that."

"The compassion. Gandhi's got nothing on you."

"I'm sure Mahatma would have agreed, why throw out perfectly good coke? It's not my cup of tea, so to speak, but waste not want not."

"You are totally like, a paragon of virtue. I bet you compost and everything."

"I am not that saintly. But I do recycle. It's the law. Anyway, that afternoon, I met Barney, and I knew he'd like it, so I let him have it."

"You let him have it, all right. But how did you know it was 'perfectly good coke'? Did you taste it? Try a little yourself? Maybe do a melting-point test like the college kid from *The French Connection*?"

"I haven't touched that stuff in ten, fifteen years. But it looked flaky and rocky, shiny white crystals, *da kine*, not that yellow Parmesan cheese crap the high school kids do."

She stood up and waved her arms around. "For crying out loud, you don't even know it was blow! You find a vial of white powder *and* a spike and a spoon, and you figure it's cocaine? What kind of dope are you? It was dope!"

"Huh? Dope? You mean like pot?"

"Dope, horse, smack, *manteca*, the big H. Heroin, stupid!"

"But you said it was coke, cut with arsenic! Now you're saying it's heroin?"

She shrugged her shoulders and sat back down. "What do I know? I'm just speculating."

"I'm no angel, but this is out of my comfort zone. I see white powder I figure cocaine, you know? I mean, what kind of deviant messes around with needles in this day and age? Haven't they heard about AIDS and Hep C for chrissakes?"

Kirsten stood up, came over by me and sat on my lap. I liked that, and was glad I wasn't standing up when she tried it, because she was heavier than she appeared. She gazed in my eye, rolled up her bathrobe sleeves and showed me her arms. The crooks of her elbows were scarred, covered with rough patches like miles of bad road.

Chapter 22

We all believe we're special. When you depart this earthly plane, unless you're a total slimeball, a bunch of people will come to your funeral. Maybe some of them—maybe a lot of them—don't even like you, but they know if they don't come to your burial, you won't go to theirs. Perhaps, if you're especially blessed, a few dozen folks will be brokenhearted when you shuffle off to Buffalo. Most of them will get over it in a year or so. Will anyone recall your passing, with great sadness, 20 or 30 years from now? Maybe an immediate family member or three. Or not. And in 100 years? Unless you're famous, fuggedaboutit. Even if you are remembered, those future people won't be sad, because who's sad about somebody dying 100 years ago? No, people will *celebrate* your death with posts on MySpace, or whatever the kids are up to in the 22nd century. A pretty morbid line of thought, but I couldn't help it—having wild sex with a stranger always makes me maudlin. Especially when, shortly after the deed, you discover your new partner has track marks up and down her arms that would put Keith Richards to shame. And, since she assured you she can't get knocked up, you didn't use a condom.

"I'm not sure, uh, how much I'm, er, what I'm supposed what to think about that. What the hell?"

"I told you I ran with a motorcycle gang doing meth."

"Yeah, but…" I pointed at the intertwining cicatrices on her arm.

"Dude, you know what you call someone who snorts heroin?"

"No, what?"

"A square."

"Very funny. But what about me?"

"What?"

"I mean, what we did, isn't that, uh, risky?"

"Not to worry, like I told you, I can't get pregnant." She put her hand around the back of my neck and smiled. I think I tried to smile back but I'm not sure how my face held up. "Oh c'mon, I'm kidding. It's safe, I don't have anything. I've been tested up and down the ying-yang."

I felt a huge wave of relief wash over me, a cleansing, calming wave. But I didn't see the rogue wave right behind it, which packed a wallop. "That's good, I guess. I'm glad your ying-yang checks out. But…you're a junkie."

"I *was* a junkie. Now I'm an *addict*."

She'd given me plenty of clues, but I'd ignored them. Finally, the penny dropped. "Ah, you're one of those."

"One of what?"

"Twelve steppers."

"Sorry, I'm not allowed to say. It's an anonymous program."

This little chippy had trouble written all over her with a capital "T" like Tiburon, which rhymes with methadon. Damaged goods. And here I am, a sucker for a scratch-and-dent discount. Hopefully she wasn't lying about being virus-free. Addicts are known to lie sometimes, aren't they? But she was funny, I had to give her that. Plus rich. I liked that part too. I didn't have a job, I didn't have a car, and I didn't have anywhere to go anyway, so I figured I'd stick around and see how this played out. That reminded me, what the heck happened to my car? How come Sean hadn't called?

"How about you? Any dark secrets I should know about?"

"The usual. I drink too much, I cheat on my taxes, I bullshit my clients an inch short of fraud. Oh yeah, and I was married once."

"Yeah? You're braver than me. What happened?"

I shrugged. "Let's just say, before I got hitched, I thought girls didn't fart and enjoyed watching sports."

"Gotcha."

This was getting too close to home; I wasn't ready—not yet, anyway—to get too intimate with Kirsten, who was hot, wealthy, but also obviously not playing with a full Tarot deck. Time to change the subject. "Explain me once more, if things are so tight you had to get a job, where'd you get the boodle to bail me out?"

"Good night nurse, haven't you figured it out yet, you big dope? *Nobody bailed you out*," she said, sparking another American Spirit. I tilted my head up and she stuck her butt in my lips and lit another one for herself. I was finding it incredibly easy to start smoking again, even though these all-natural cigs tasted lousy, but I'd have had to walk over a mile from her house if I wanted a Camel, so I just kept smoking them. "The morning after Barney died, the cops went down to his construction site to poke around. But the construction worker who fingered you for giving Barney the drugs? Surprise! Turns out he's undocumented. He flew the coop right after he snitched. Probably halfway to Guatemala by now."

"I get it. The cops had nothing to hold me on."

"That's right, Einstein. Not till they get the lab results back. They called the office when they were ready to kick you loose. I wasn't doing anything, so I picked you up."

"But we barely know each other. I mean, now we know each other, a little bit anyway, but why…"

"Rilly? How many times I gotta say it, I'm bored! I want to have fun! All I do is watch TV and exercise and do yoga and go to meetings and try not to eat too many sweets. Work is even worse…selling houses sucks, dude, I don't know how you can handle it. All you do is hang around waiting for some rich jerk to give you money for nothing."

I didn't understand. She was awfully bitter about our shared profession after having put in what, one day's work? I mean, her analysis was spot on—the job mostly *was* doing nothing, hanging around, and waiting for people to give you money for it—but that's exactly why it was so great. It was my dream job. Why was she complaining? Women. Am I right?

Chapter 23

My Treo buzzed. Had to be Sean. Finally. "Excuse me, I better take this," I said to Kirsten as I wriggled out from under her and stood up. My legs had fallen asleep, so I had to put a hand on the granite countertop to keep from teetering. My dick had fallen asleep too, which, believe it or not, happens sometimes. I guess he was tired. I would have rubbed him to get the blood flowing again but I didn't want Kirsten to get the right idea. I held up a finger as I put the cellphone to my ear, implying permission to take the call. Can you believe how primitive we were back then? We actually asked people around us if it was OK if stopped speaking to them to talk on our phones.

"Rick Davies?"

"Speaking."

"This is Detective Keyes. You remember me, I'm the fellow who tased you yesterday."

"Oh sure, hi Detective, how are you?" California nice. I turned to Kirsten and mouthed "It's the cops!" Her eyes opened wide.

"Good, you?"

"Not bad. Just had a healthy salad. It had kale in it."

"Kale? That's good for you right?"

"It better be." Enough small talk. Nobody in California ever says how they're feeling, or what they're really thinking. We talk about what we ate, or a hike we went on, snow conditions at Tahoe, the latest hot tech stock, or our dog. It was like that old cartoon, the New Yorker and the Californian shaking hands across the continent. The New Yorker is saying "Screw you!" but a thought balloon shows that he's really thinking, "Hey, how you doing?" while the Californian is saying "Hey, how you doing?" but he's really thinking, "Screw you!"

"What can I do you for, Detective?"

"Do you know a Mr. Sean Whitehead?"

"Sure, he's my downstairs neighbor. Swell guy."

"Did you know he had your car?"

"Of course, I lent it to him. What's this all about?"

"Sean was on his way to Muir Beach to meet a client and he took a wrong turn."

"Oh yeah, he kept going on Montford instead of turning right up the hill onto Molino. People do that all the time."

"No, not that one. On the road down from the 1."

"Is he lost?"

"He might have been, but now he's found. It was about a 200-foot drop. Sean is dead."

"Fu..., I mean, shucks, that's terrible news." I assumed my Beemer was totaled. I still had two years on the lease, and I hoped my insurance would cover it.

"Yes. I've noticed, terrible news seems to follow in your footsteps. Marjorie Khan, Barney, now Sean. Say, if you're not busy, we'd like you to come downtown and answer a few questions."

"What's that? I'm about to go through the Waldo Tunnel, I think I'm gonna lose you." I hung up.

"What did he want?"

I'd seen that TV show *The Wire* (it's really good, you should watch it if you haven't already) so I knew to turn off my phone and remove its battery while I was on the lam. So that's what I did. "They want me to come to the station and answer some questions."

"Agin? Those guys are such a buzz kill. What did he say? You're pale as a ghost."

"Sean, my neighbor. I borrowed him my car yesterday morning." Was it only yesterday morning? So much had happened since then, it felt much longer. And what the hell, now I was starting to speak like him, mixing up "borrowed" and "lent." What is it with Minnesotans?

"Today he drove it off a cliff."

"Dang."

A not uncomfortable silence passed between us. "I've been thinking?"

"Why start now?"

"Shecky Green over here. But isn't the timing weird? Just when we might have tumbled onto something. Whoever planted the poison blow or dope or whatever it was, maybe now they're coming for me."

"I get the picture—you got the frame. That it?"

"It's a helluva coincidence, no?"

"Where are you going with this?"

"Maybe somebody cut the brake cables on my car."

She leaned forward over the marble countertop, affording me a quick glimpse of her cleavage. Man, I didn't want any trouble with the heat, murderers, car crashes or dope fiends, I just wanted to dive in that soft white cavern and never come out. "Oh, wow, you mean like, on TV?"

"I don't know much about how cars work, just like the upholstery and sound systems and wheels and finish. But yeah."

"This is getting nutty. You know what we oughta do?"

"Yeah," I said, reaching down into her bathrobe.

She slapped my hand away. "No time to get into all of that now. We gotta talk to Mrs. Papadopoulos before the po-po get to her. Find out just what's up with the what-what."

"Great idea." We both looked at my phone, its battery out and its cover off. Was I being paranoid, or not careful enough? Should I have put the phone in the microwave, or run it through the garbage disposal?

Kirsten held up a palm and said, "I got this. Besides, I have a better rapport with Mrs. P than you do."

I thought I had a great relationship with Mrs. P, but I let it slide. I was too scared to use my phone, so there was no point in arguing. Kirsten reached into her purse and pulled out a gleaming black metal gadget.

"What is that thing, some kinda new Blackberry?"

"Pfft. Blackberries suck. How 2006. It's an iPhone. It eats Blackberries for breakfast."

Now I recognized it—it was the same posh dealy-o Barney had, and Detective Keyes too. Was I the last person in Marin not to have one? "Oh yeah, those are cool, can I see it?" I reached out and she spun away.

"No. It's brand-new and I love it. Now shut up and let me make the call."

I watched her dial the number, using her finger instead of a stylus. It was like looking into the future, and I wondered again how I could get rid of my Treo and get me one of those i-thingies. Maybe if I said it was in the car when Sean crashed it, insurance would cover it and Verizon would let me out of my contract. A man can dream, can't he?

Chapter 24

It was getting late and, despite Kirsten's sweet talking, Mrs. P respectfully declined to rendezvous with us that night. She was watching some geriatric murder mystery on TV and couldn't rip herself away. Kirsten made arrangements to get together the next day. Kirsten was crafty, acting coy, like there was some positive development with the house that was too delicate to discuss over the phone. Mrs. P, like everyone selling an empty house for which they were still paying heating, electricity and property taxes, wanted the damn thing sold yesterday, so she bought Kirsten's pitch hook, line and sinker. Kirsten was good. She didn't even drop any real hints, just a few artfully placed keywords, and let Mrs. P imagine she was hearing what she wanted to hear, fill in the blanks the way she wanted. Then again I suppose we all do that. So of course Mrs. P agreed to see us. Not us, that is—she agreed to meet Kirsten, my name wasn't brought up. I found this demeaning—this was my listing after all. But I remembered I didn't have a job anymore, never mind any listings, so Kirsten was clever to keep it on the down low—it was surely better not to tell Mrs. P that the guy who got pinched at her open house that morning would be tagging along. Kirsten hung up and put her cool phone back in her chic bag.

"Man, I need a drink."

"Dude! Me too, but I'm not ginna have one."

"Huh?"

"I'm not gonna have one. But it makes me feel better to admit I want one."

"It makes me feel better when I have one. Whaddya got?"

"Here? Nothing. I told you, I don't drink."

Had she? I forget. She told me she didn't do drugs anymore. But ex-addicts can still drink, right? I mean, how could they not?

"Not even a glass of wine with dinner?"

"You see me having a glass of wine with dinner, best you start running the other way."

"Seriously. You don't have anything here at all? Not a drop? An Ativan, maybe? Not even any weed?"

"Nope! But I can see you need something." She tried to frown and got about halfway there. "I can call my massage therapist, she makes virtual Reiki house calls. Or maybe you need cranial-sacral work, to overcome birth trauma?"

I stared back at her.

"Oh all right, ya big baby. Let me get you some shoes." I'd already tossed my Bruno Maglis, they were shot. She scurried back to the bedroom and returned momentarily with a pair of white patent-leather shoes. I could tell she was enjoying this.

"What, no Captain's hat?"

"Your head's too big."

"Bummer. I wanted to capture the full L. Ron Hubbard effect."

We headed over to the Safeway in Strawberry. I don't care what Allen Ginsberg said: me, I love supermarkets in California. They're open late and they sell not just beer and wine but hard stuff, too. When I was a kid, you could only buy beer at the liquor store, and they were closed on Sundays. That's right, you couldn't buy beer on Sundays. How crazy is that? Anyway, I didn't know when I'd be able to get back to a package store (as we used to call them in Rhode Island), or anyplace else for that matter, so I figured I'd better stock up. I snagged a fifth of Bushmills (Black Bush; highly recommended), a bottle of Glenlivet, a quart of Tanqueray, a half-gallon plastic jug of cheap tequila with a picture of a mariachi musician on the label (was it the same guy I'd sold the house to in Petaluma?), and some lemons and limes to maintain healthy vitamin C levels and ward off scurvy.

Kirsten clearly disapproved, but didn't say anything, which I appreciated.

Meanwhile, she picked up a packet of dried seaweed, some ginseng cookies, a half-gallon of cold-pressed carrot juice and a quart of Rice Dream ice cream. But she also grabbed two 64-oz bottles of Diet Coke, a family-size bag of Cool Ranch Doritos, Chips Ahoy, Double Stuff Oreos, a quart of Cherry Garcia, and a carton of American Spirits. Etiquette demanded I follow her lead and not question her choices, at least some of which were arguably worse than mine, but I found it more than passing strange that half of her snack predilections were the polar opposite of our earlier repast.

"Um, I'm no expert, but, don't Doritos have, I'm assuming, GMOs, but also like all sorts of toxic Babylon shitstem sort of crap in 'em?"

"Oh, it's OK, it's my new diet. I eat nothing but raw food all day but then at night I can have whatever I want. My friend Nancy, she told me about it. She's an Ashtanga yoga teacher. She's also a Breatharian, but that regime is too strict for me."

"Breatharian?"

"Yeah, they don't eat or drink, just get all the nutrients they need from fresh air and sunshine. But it's a pain 'cause you have to be touching Mother Earth barefoot for like four hours a day."

Shows what I get for asking questions.

At the checkout line, I magnanimously offered to put it all on my credit card. It was a company card. I figured I'd keep using it till it stopped working. Kirsten saw what I was doing and tried to raise an eyebrow, but kept her trap shut. The checkout guy asked her for ID; she liked that.

We walked back out to the parking lot. I carried both bags full of goodies. It was cold and windy. "Now let's go watch some TV," she said. My kinda gal.

We got back to Kirsten's palace on the hill and I lugged our treats to the home theater—of course there was a home theater, totally tricked out. The room had half-a-dozen old-timey leather club chairs facing a

Panasonic plasma TV, just like mine, only hers had a ginormous 65" screen. I felt ashamed of my relatively paltry 37 inches, and vowed to go bigger as soon as I got another job.

"You ever watch *Friday Night Lights*?"

"I saw the first season, it was pretty good, but I haven't gotten around to season two yet."

"Perfect, I haven't seen season two yet either, but I've got it all on my TiVo."

TiVo? People still had those? What was wrong with the standard DVR our friends at Comcast gave us? We sat there drinking and watching TV; I was enjoying my Bushmills, which was delicious if you don't mind my saying so, while she guzzled Diet Coke. "You really don't drink?" I asked her. "That's crazy."

"Tell me about it. Believe you me—me and alcohol? A bad combination." I flashed back to a very nice combination I'd shown her just a few hours earlier.

"I don't get it. Why can't you drink? I thought you had a drug problem."

"I have a life problem." She stuffed a handful of Cool Ranch Doritos in her pie hole, rendering her pretty mouth a bright orange rictus.

I believed her. "You and me both, kid," I said, pouring a couple more fingers onto the half-melted ice cubes in my glass.

We watched a few episodes, all in a row, the TiVo automagically removing commercials. Now I understood why she paid an extra fee above and beyond her cable box. It was a fun way to watch TV. Amazing the way rich people live. The show had gone way downhill since I'd last tuned in. There was a ridiculous storyline about one of the football kids, the nerdy one with blond hair, with the face that belonged in one of those big bell jars they used to have at the freak show at Coney Island, hooking up with the beautiful slutty blonde cheerleader, and then accidentally murdering some guy who was stalking her. What the hell, where did that come from? You've got a show about teenagers, with realistic portrayals of their relationships with each other and their families, an empathetic view of parents coping with their crazy hormonal kids (and each other), engaging, emotionally and intellectually profound, and out of left field, they throw in a murder because the insightful social commentary wasn't interesting enough. I suppose the ratings weren't as high as the muckety-mucks expected, so they had to do something to titillate the hoi polloi. What bullshit. I was disgusted. I felt used, duped. I took another swig of Black Bush, then sucked on an ice cube. The booze-infused cube felt good in my mouth.

"Hey, enough for me, I'm ready for bed. You?" I smiled and did a Groucho Marx invitation with my eyebrows. I desperately wanted her to accompany me, but had somehow managed to hang on to enough self-esteem to not make a direct proposition.

"I'm good," she said, not averting her gaze from the screen. She apparently liked the show more than I did. Or maybe she just liked it more than she liked me. Which was depressing because the show stunk on ice, even half-melted whiskey ice. She lifted an arm and pointed, like God reaching out to Adam, still watching the TV and barely paying me any attention. "Guestroom's down that way, second door on your right."

"Thanks again. I mean, I don't know how I can thank you for all you've done…"

"Go to your room and shut the door, that's all the thanks I need," she intoned blankly, eyes still glued to the TV.

I sidled off, feeling the way I've felt most of my life as I've gone to bed alone: confused, disappointed and horny.

Chapter 25

I'd gotten tipsy the night before, and passed out listening to Beethoven's Sixth Symphony; the humongous "guestroom" had a better stereo than my home system, which I'm usually proud of, and a wall of CDs. I'm not a big classical fan but the Sixth never fails to put me to sleep, so I love it. I hadn't drunk nearly as much as I wanted to; I was hoping Kirsten would throw me another bone so I stayed relatively sober. What a waste. End result, I woke up early, around 7:30 a.m., with raging morning wood. If I ever got another crack at Kirsten, and hoped to make a decent second impression, I couldn't let myself get backed up like this. A quick wank was in order to clean out the pipes and get my heart started. I began by thinking about Kirsten, but somehow that didn't feel right, so I switched to my ex-wife, what it was like in the beginning, but that quickly led me to remember what it was like in the middle so that didn't work either. I thought about Jessica Alba, Natalie Portman and Scarlett Johansson, but the celebrity thing wasn't happening. I dug deep into the memory banks and remembered the time I'd almost had a three-way with my college girlfriend and her best friend before we'd all chickened out. I locked in, focused like a laser beam and the next thing I had an embarrassing mess to deal with. As Martin Luther said, if it doesn't go into a woman, it goes into your shirt.

Fortunately, the guestroom Kirsten had exiled me to was in a separate wing of the house and had its own bathroom, so I could dispose of the shameful onanistic evidence in private. The bathroom was half the size of my house. Whirlpool tub, his-and-her sinks and a shower stall. Whoa, was that a Silvertag? Damn, 120k for a shower head. And a plasma TV on the wall, a 42" Panasonic, in case you didn't feel like reading while you sat on the Japanese washlet. Good thing I'd beaten off before I came in here, 'cause this was making me feel limp.

I hung yesterday's clothes on a $250 chrome towel bar from Restoration Hardware. The steam from the shower would act as a makeshift iron and her dad's duds wouldn't look as disheveled as I felt. I rummaged through the medicine cabinet, hoping for T3s, or at least some Advil Cold & Sinus. I found aspirin, chewed a couple and placed the bitter granules under my tongue. I missed my dad's morphine; I was sad I'd never see that pretty brown bottle ever again. Chuckleheaded Sean. Story of my life, do somebody a favor and take it up the poop chute.

I stepped into the swanky shower stall, lined floor to ceiling with imported Florentine tile. The lukewarm water softly raining down from the shower head hurt my hair less than usual; I supposed the Silvertag was worth it, if you could afford it. Then again, what isn't?

I dried off with a fluffy Egyptian cotton towel, thread count over 1000, just like the sheets I'd slid into after Kirsten told me to go tuck myself. Talk about cold comfort. Nice and clean, on the outside at least, I donned the white safari getup and admired myself in a full-length mirror. Ricardo Montalban had nothing on me. I slowly let the syllables "Cor-do-ba" triple off my lips. Who's got it going on?

I padded my way back to the kitchen/great room. Kirsten was doing yoga. Yogis work as hard as coal miners used to. She pulled and stretched and contorted her splendid and reasonably well-proportioned body. Her muscles rippled as she worked, like a beautiful overheated sweaty beast of burden, and the room was filled with a ripe spiritual odor.

She regarded me, upside down through her legs, as I entered the room, saying, "Good morning, sunshine." She put her hands on her knees and gracefully lifted her torso upright and wiped off her pure goddess perspiration with a towel.

"Hey, don't quit on my account."

"It's OK, I'm just about done, and I don't need you staring at my *mula bandha*. You want breakfast?"

"Food? Sure, I like food. And hey, thanks again for letting me crash here last night."

"De nada." She sat down at the Reef table and pointed at the huge built-in Sub Zero. "Eggs, bacon, bread, all in there. Help yourself."

Eggs. Bacon. Bread. My ass. We'd been through this already, and once was enough. "Maybe I'll just have some fruit." There was a large bowl full of all sorts of colorful fruits on the table in front of her.

"Got plenty of that." She grabbed a banana, peeled it and started eating it, gazing deeply into my eyes. Good thing I'd jacked off already. "You want coffee? I just made a pot." There was a huge machine on the counter top, all steel and glass and copper tubing. One of the tubes was slowly dripping caramel-colored liquid into a carafe underneath the Rube Goldberg apparatus.

"You? Drink coffee? I thought you were on the holy path of my body is a temple and all that. At least during the day."

She shrugged. "Coffee's all I got left. You wanna take it from me, you'll have to pry it from my hot, twitchy fingers."

I poured myself a cup. "I'm assuming this is shade-grown fair-trade and dolphin-free?"

"It's Kopi Luwak. You know, cat scat coffee."

The cup was almost at my lips and I stopped short. "Come again?"

"Really? You haven't heard of it? It's from Indonesia. See, they have these wild cats there called civets, they're kinda like house cats but they're like twice as big. Anyway, these cats are coo-coo for coffee beans, so people follow them around and collect their droppings and they scoop out what's left of the partially digested beans. It's the only kind I'll drink. Costs about $1000 a pound, so drink up."

Lecture complete, she picked up her *Marin IJ* off the table, opened it up and disappeared behind it. $1000 a pound? I better try it. I'd never had a $50 cup of coffee before. Or a $50 cup of cat shit, for that matter. I thought maybe I better sweeten it.

"Sugar?"

"In the jar right in front of you, and milk's in the fridge."

Knowing the milk wouldn't really be milk, I skipped it and filled up a spoon with sugar. I should have known; of course it wasn't sugar, it was obviously yet another fugazi, too powdery. "This isn't real sugar, is it?"

"Stevia, it's the latest substitute. It's great. I won't use anything else."

"Yeah, Splenda is nasty, gives you migraines."

"And NutraSweet gives you brain tumors, and saccharine causes cancer. That's why I'm on Stevia."

Why is it that every former drunk I've ever met eats more sugar than a hyperactive fourth-grader the day after Halloween, until it gets it into their head that sugar's worse than meth, so instead they pound down whatever faddish sweet chemical is currently popular? I didn't say anything; it's a waste of time trying to talk people out of their personal insanities. Trying two new things at once was too much to bear, especially before I'd had any coffee, so I put the spoon back down and took a sip of my $50 coffee, black. It was OK.

"What with the track record, don't you think they'll find something awful about Stevia someday too?"

"No doubt. And until that day, I will drink the living crap out of it."

Chapter 26

It was a beautiful day. As per usual. Sunny, 72 degrees, not a cloud in the sky, a refreshing zephyr blowing in off Richardson Bay. Back East, you get 18, maybe 20 days a year this lovely. When it's like this in New York City, working stiffs take long lunches, if they don't skip work altogether, the girls are barely dressed and everybody's in a great mood. Here, it's like this more often than not, 200 days or so a year, so nobody cares.

Kirsten emerged from the four-door garage in yet another car. This time it was a Prius. I hopped in the front seat. "Really?" I couldn't believe she could stand to drive this piece of junk after the M6—it's like a $12,000 Hyundai with a $15,000 battery. It's the car for people who hate cars, the car that sucks all possible joy out of driving. "Feeling guilty about destroying the planet?"

"Not really. I was at an Adyashanti seminar recently? And some kid in tie-dye and patchouli complained about his parents not caring about the environment, and he asked Adya what he should do about their pig-headedness, and Adya said, 'How do you know they're doing anything wrong? It *seems* like it's wrong to drive a giant SUV and burn up what's left of the world's dwindling fossil fuel supply and contribute to global warming. It *seems* wrong to me too. But what do I know? Maybe it just *seems* that way. Maybe it's exactly what the planet needs to have happen—for us to run out of oil sooner rather than later. Doesn't make much sense, but I don't know—you don't know either. Nobody knows!'"

"So why do you drive this heap when you have an M6?"

"Good for the new job. Makes a better impression on clients. You know, show 'em I'm green and thrifty. Seems the expected Al Qaeda invasion isn't happening and Hummers are going out of style."

"Yeah, where's John Walker Lindh now that we need him?"

I wondered what else was in that seemingly endless garage. A DeLorean, a Bentley, a mint condition Stutz Bearcat? Or maybe, like most of the houses I saw, Kirsten used her garage as a giant storage bin, and it was packed with piles of musty books, complete runs of '60s *National Geographics*, 8-track players, useless turntables and vinyl records, black-and-white TVs and VHS tapes, out-of-style clothes that didn't fit anymore and never would again—the typical 20th-century detritus I wade through for estate sales.

Right, estate sales. That's how this mess all started. Probably better if I don't dredge Kirsten's garage; I'd probably find something I didn't want to. Everybody's got a lost tortoise of some kind. We silently descended the winding streets till we reached Tiburon Boulevard. The way the Prius didn't make any noise creeped me out. Supposedly a lot of blind people have been run over by Priuses because you can't hear them coming.

We hung a Roscoe and headed over to The Ghetto, as the swells in Tiburon refer to Mill Valley. Tiburon was where the wealthy lived; folks in Mill Valley are just rich. You know what the difference is between rich and wealthy? Rich people buy courtside seats at Warriors games. Wealthy people own the Warriors. Everything's relative, I guess. Mill Valley *is* a ghetto of sorts. Sure there were loads of new, upscale McMansions, but it was still peppered with plenty of unrestored teardowns, many of them still occupied by burnt-out leftover hippies who paid ten grand for their hovel 40 years ago. The present-day buyers are banking on getting their own massive payoff. I mean, why else would a couple making $300k a year between them take on an $10-grand-a-month mortgage, willingly become house poor, if they weren't sure their $2-million-dollar ranch house wasn't going to be worth $10 million in a decade or two? Prices were going up 25% a year, and prices never go down, not in Southern Marin, it's a one-way rocket ship to the moon! That's what I told my clients, and they believed me, because, just like Fox Mulder, they wanted to believe. Hey, if they don't understand compound interest, believe trees grow to the sky and in trickle-down economics, that's not my fault. Who am I to talk people out of their delusions, if it makes them happy? Where would we be without our delusions?

We cruised past Blackie's Pasture, with the life-size bronze sculpture of the eponymous horse who once grazed there. Blackie was a former cavalry horse who fed in this very field for 28 years until his death in 1966. The Tiburonites never got over it, and erected a statue in his honor in 1995. I find this fascinating—I heard that sociopaths reserve their minimal feelings for babies and animals. I don't know why—low stakes? If it's true that behind every great fortune is a great crime, that meant there were a lot of criminals in Tiburon. Not street outlaws prone to violence, but crooks nonetheless, and most crooks are sociopaths, so it made sense that these monied entitletarians would memorialize a horse that had been dead for 30 years instead of one of their more famous human scions, say Pat Paulson, Mariel Hemingway, Eve Arden or Courtney-Thorne Smith.

We crossed the 101 and entered Mill Valley proper. Tiburon turns into Mill Valley half a mile or so before the highway, but that neighborhood is known as Strawberry, and friends don't let friends live in Strawberry, though I've sold my fair share of Kott houses there. Better than Novato, I guess. Novato is the worst place in the world, a scorched earth, post-apocalyptic wasteland overrun by mutant freaks. Better you should live in Somalia. You know what Novato means in Spanish? "Don't go to." At least that's how folks in Southern Marin feel about it.

Another thing. I don't know why they call it "the 101" instead of "101," like we would on the East Coast, or maybe even "route 101," but they do. They put a "the" in front of all the highways, like "Take THE 101 to THE 280, then get on THE 85…" or whatever. Another Californian unsolved mystery.

No surprise, a traffic jam. As we crawled over the bridge, I saw what was causing the backup—a mattress in the middle lane of the northbound 101. How much can a used mattress cost from Goodwill? Fifty bucks? Tops? And you know they've cleaned and fumigated it. Why then do I constantly see old beater cars—usually a rust-bucket vintage Accord—packed with riffraff, with a mattress precariously tied to the top? Who in their right mind would take a used mattress from somebody and tie it to their roof? On the other hand, Mitt Romney once tied his dog to the roof of his car, and he might be president some day, so who knows why people do what they do? For God's sake, there are people out there who prefer Journey to the Dead, like Chicago-style deep-dish pizza more than coal oven, and think *Rescue Me* is better than *Deadwood*. But haven't these mattress-carting dopes heard about the bedbug epidemic? I wish at least somebody had been a boy scout, so they'd learned how to tie a damn knot and the mattresses wouldn't fall willy nilly on the highway all the goddamn time. If you listen to the traffic reports on AM 720, you'll hear at least once a week: "Mattress obstruction on the 101." As if the highways weren't messed up enough already. Bay Area traffic is terrible, and it's especially bad in Mill Valley, as there are only three ways out of town, and they're all single lane. Rush hour is a nightmare. We all have our crosses to bear.

The street narrowed from two lanes to one as we made our way onto East Blithedale, right before the Chevron station. A black SUV sidled up on our left, not slowing down to let us pass, or speeding up to get ahead of us. Kirsten had to lay on the brakes so we didn't get run off the road. I opened my window, stuck my middle finger up high and gave it a spinning motion so the douchebag could see how I felt about his driving. A Lexus. What did I tell you?

"Jesus, road rage much?" Kirsten asked as I slumped back into my seat.

"He cut us off!"

"So what?"

"It's my civic duty to let him know he's an asshole."

"I'm sure he knows already. People are very self-aware in this town, what with all the therapy, meditation and self-improvement courses. It's barely noon and you've already crossed paths with one asshole. You know what they say."

I didn't want to ask who "they" were. "What?"

"If you run into more than three assholes in a day, you're one of them."

I'd have to remember that. It didn't really make sense, but it sort of did. Good line to drop at a cocktail party. It occurred to me that Kirsten was being kind of an asshole. That made two today already. I'd better watch my step.

Chapter 27

"We still have an hour before we're meeting Mrs. Papadopoulos. Wanna grab a bite?"

"I could eat." After a couple of Kirsten's health meals, I was dying for some fried greasy carbs, so at my urging we popped into the Mexican place off East Blithedale, next to the gardening store. I ordered chimichangas, which can be hard to find in California, as they're not real Mexican food, but Tex-Mex. Kirsten had an iceberg lettuce salad, no dressing. Mort Sahl and Robin Williams sat down at the table next to ours and everybody pretended they didn't notice. I'm not sure about Kirsten's salad, but my chimichangas were OK, nothing to write home about. Most food is great in the Bay Area. You know why? Ask anybody, they're happy to tell you: ingredients. There's a good chance they'll tell you even if you don't ask. But for some reason, most of the restaurants in Mill Valley—most of Marin for that matter—are terribly mediocre, or worse. Just 15 miles away, in the Mission, you can get the best burrito in the country. Even closer, in Chinatown, there's Chinese joints so good that businessmen from Beijing make a point of stopping by when they're in town. In the East Bay, there's your Chez Panisse, and up north in Napa it's the French Laundry and Michelin stars galore. I don't know why, but you enter a culinary dark timeline when you drive over the Golden Gate Bridge. The ethnic food is, I dunno, what's the word, deracinated? It's like the chefs just don't care. And it costs twice, maybe three times as much as in the city. Maybe it's 'cause we're a captive audience. Nobody likes to leave Marin, if they can help it.

I don't know if the rumor that Carlos Santana owned this hash house was true, but they were playing *Santana's Greatest Hits* on a loop the whole time we were there. Santana's not so bad, not as bad as he sounds, anyway, but I find it déclasseé to play your own records at your own establishment, much the same way I find it distasteful when homeowners paper their walls with family photographs. I get it, you live here, and this is your family, but do you really like seeing so much of yourself? Me, I can barely stand checking myself out when I pass by a mirror, because I no longer look like I did when I was 26, which is somehow what I still expect to see. Somebody, I can't remember who, once said, "Mirrors and copulation are abominable, since they both multiply the numbers of men..." I hate mirrors, but copulation is A-OK in my book. Nobody's right all the time.

Anyway, a friend of mine who grew up here told me back in the '60s Santana used to busk on the streets of Sausalito, doing the same shtick—the funny faces, dueling congas and piercing riffs—that made him world famous at Woodstock a couple of years later. Sausalito was a hoot back in the day. The notorious madam Sally Stanford ran a brothel in the city for 50 years, frequented by Teddy Kennedy, among many other notables. She became mayor of Sausalito in 1975. They used to have an unwritten rule: the law stopped at the water. Sausalito has 400 or so houseboats, many of them slapped together from subchasers and other Navy boats boats abandoned after World War II, when they decommissioned the Marinship shipyards. They used the old hulls and built makeshift houses on top. Most of them are louche, musty health hazards that couldn't pass a safety inspection but are grandfathered in. In the '60s and '70s they were full of hippies, bikers, new-agers, porn stars, drug traffickers and other practitioners of alternative lifestyles. I'll leave it to your imagination what went on past the water's edge. Nowadays you get a speeding ticket so fast it'll make your head spin if you go a mile over 30 on Bridgeway.

We drove past the Methodist church on Camino Alto. Today their outdoor signboard read: "Jesus had two dads and he turned out fine." We continued past the Safeway—not the Safeway in Strawberry where we bought the booze and snacks, the other one—and the entrance to the

Redwoods, a nursing home for the well-to-do, on the left. That's where Mrs. P hung her hat.

"Hey, you just missed it."

"It's Friday afternoon, she won't be in her room."

Tam High was letting out early for some reason, and we had to stop while the poor kids without their own Beemers and Mercedes meandered over to the Safeway parking lot where Mom was waiting in the Range Rover. I inspected the unlined faces of the disaffected rich youths, the leaders of the next generation, in their larval state. Well-dressed, well-fed, well-behaved kids. Half of them medicated, they walked into the traffic like zombies, trusting that the drivers were paying attention. Who could blame them for being depressed, growing up in this sterile burg, with the self-involved, self-evolved, Ted-Talk-loving parents they probably had? As good a time as any to mention that the original *Invasion of the Body Snatchers* was set in Mill Valley. Made me sad. See, I believe that children are the future. But I didn't see anybody here who would turn out interesting when they grew up—no prospective Anton LaVeys, Tupac Shakurs, John Cipollinas or even Mario Cipollinas—all Tam High alums. But you never know. Maybe those guys all looked like carefree dopes when they went to school here too.

We hung a Huey by the high school and headed back up Miller. About 40 oldsters were gathered on the corner of Miller and Camino Alto, holding signs that said "US Out of Iraq," "Give Peace a Chance," "Support the Troops: Bring Them Home," and even "Down Down Bush," which I thought was only used in Middle Eastern countries we were about to invade, but I applaud diversity when I see it.

The seniors hooted and hollered as we rolled up to the stoplight, flashing wide grins and peace signs. Were these real, unreconstructed hippies, I wondered, or people who got cool when they turned 70? Their kids, maybe even their grandkids, were out of college, so they sold the family homestead, made a bundle and were now living it up in a luxury retirement home, nothing to do but chill out and drink, smoke weed, and screw. Thank God for Viagra! And the best part of all, you didn't have to worry about birth control! So of course nobody used condoms, and STDs ran rampant through communities like this. What the hell, you only live once, and these folks had done most of their living already, may as well go out with a bang.

"Octavia!" Kirsten called out.

Mrs. Papadopoulos, holding a sign that read, "GMO Labelling Now!" turned toward us and lit up when she saw Kirsten. Then she saw me and scowled, handed the sign to a fellow gray-haired monied malcontent, leaned on the window and said, "Ah, you. What an unexpected pleasure." Refreshing sarcasm from a native. Most home-grown folks out here don't get sarcasm. Are they naturally non-cynical, or is it just an East Coast thing?

She climbed in the back seat and kicked mine hard enough to hurt my spine. She caught Kirsten's eye in the rear-view mirror. "What's this clown doing here?" Honesty—even more startling. How invigorating!

Chapter 28

My job, more than most, depends on relationships. I'm required by law to be a fiduciary, whatever that means. I establish a personal tie with my clients, forge a bond. Apparently, getting collared at a client's open house has a deleterious effect on said bond. Happily I'm as good at patching up connections gone bad as I am making new ones—practice makes perfect.

I swiveled to face Mrs. P in the back seat. "Hey, I didn't go to four years of clown college to get treated this way." That got a small chuckle out of her. A crack in the façade. I knew I could win her back.

"Shall we go get a cup of coffee?" Kirsten asked. She was a helluva diplomat. Typical of kids whose parents fought a lot.

"Let's go to the Depot. Wilmer will be there, I want him to be part of this meeting."

"Wilmer?" I said.

"My nephew, Wilmer Bentson. His father was Caleb Bentson—you're in real estate, you must have heard of him."

Of course. Caleb Bentson was before my time, but he was a local legend. King of the teardowns.

"Wilmer's very successful in his own right, something to do with computers, I never understood what. He's made lots of money, never any trouble with the law. You could learn a thing or two from him, Mr. Davies."

She was probably right. The light turned green and Kirsten gunned it down Miller toward downtown. "Yeah, if he's such a computer genius maybe he could show me how to organize my iTunes collection. It still puts my Dylan records under 'B,' my Bowie records under 'D' and my Stones and Beatles records under 'T.'" But seriously Mrs. Papadopoulos, I want to apologize for what happened the other day, I never intended to make a scene like that."

"Who would?"

Good point. "You realize it was a case of mistaken identity."

"Isn't it always? Such a shame your company acted so hastily, fired you without giving you the benefit of the doubt. It's almost as if something like this has happened before and they didn't feel like giving you a third chance."

Damn, how did she know about the Ross debacle? I decided to be smart for once and clam up. Of course she knew about it. This is a small town. A small town in a small county—nobody was more than a degree or two away from having a finger up their neighbor's butthole. I snuck another peek at Mrs. Papadopoulos in the back mirror. Despite her loose, deeply lined skin, I could tell from her bright hazel eyes and high cheekbones she'd been a stone fox once upon a time. I remembered she had sort of come-on to me when we'd first met. I'd still play that card if it came down to brass tacks. Sure her hair was gray, but all cats are gray sooner or later.

We passed the Baskin-Robbins; Jerry Harrison was walking out, licking an ice cream cone. Looked like pistachio. Crossing the street, we entered the Depot parking lot, passed the diagonal slots occupied by the usual panoply of luxury automobiles. We kept rolling, silently, in that eerie Prius way. Kirsten had to tap the horn a couple of times so pedestrians, who couldn't hear us otherwise, would get out the way. We couldn't find a spot. Downtown Mill Valley—too much entitlement, not enough parking. We circled around the big redwoods, passing Peets and a few stores with French-sounding names, high-class clip joints that peddle $3000 handbags, fancy hats and cruise-ship art. They only had to sell one or two per month of whatever they were fobbing off to make rent. Not that they had to make rent—some big wheel was happy to eat the difference so long as it kept his bored trophy wife out of the house. I once went into one of these stores to buy a belt. I knew it would be expensive, so I picked out the simplest one, a strip of leather with a basic square brass buckle. They wanted $150. I didn't need a belt that bad; the next day, I found the same one at Macy's at The Village at Corte Madera for $12. Not even on sale.

We ended up parking at the Mill Valley Market, dropped in a few quarters and strolled over to the Depot.

"This isn't too far, Octavia?"

"I'm old, not an invalid. And I'm not even that old." She winked at me. I repressed a shudder and smiled back.

As usual, there was a long line at the Depot. Not as bad as Starbucks when some joker orders a specialty drink, a lemongrass gazpacho espresso on ice or whatever and it takes 20 minutes, but they're no speed demons at the Depot either. Kirsten ordered a chamomile tea. I guess she really did stick to her special fecal brew. Or maybe she controlled her caffeine addiction by only drinking coffee in the morning, the same way no self-respecting drunk will drink before five. But wait, doesn't chamomile tea calm the nerves? Maybe she was combining it with her cat-shit Joe from earlier as a sort of recovery speedball. Mrs. Papadopoulos surprised me by ordering a Fat Tire. Once she blazed that trail, I followed suit, and requested the same. 1:30 p.m.—close enough. Plus a blueberry muffin. The sign said it contained 500 calories, but hey, I was hungry. I was starting to warm up to the old lady. She frowned at me.

"Copy cat." She turned back to the barista. "I'll have a blueberry muffin as well."

Yeah, she was warming up to me too.

When our order was finally ready, we tried to find an outside table. It wasn't easy. Despite some weird glitches, like that thing with Bear Stearns, and the subprime crack-up, the economy was booming. Some pusillanimous clients were worried because foreclosures were on the rise in former hotspots like Vegas, Miami and Vallejo. I put their worries to rest—this is fortress Marin! It didn't affect us if there was a bust in the

Inland Empire—our prosperity was based on the rock-solid foundation of high-tech, high-finance and high self-esteem. Some old geezer had recently bought MySpace for $750 million bones—a bargain at twice the price—bubbles were blowing like crazy and there were high-paying jobs aplenty in the Bay Area. The business mags were calling it "Tech Bubble 2.0," meaning that as a compliment, not a warning. There'd never been a better time to buy. So who were these people, lounging around in the hot afternoon sunlight, in the middle of a workday, drinking overpriced drinks, without a worry in the world, not even concerned about skin cancer?

A lot of them made a fortune during the first dot-com boom, a $5 or $10 million score when they were 30 or 35, now they're retired and do angel investing for fun and profit. Or maybe they're a little older, and cleaned up from the first tech boom in the '80s. Or was that the second tech boom? Yeah, there've been a lot of bubbles, wave after wave, and the detritus from those crashing waves washes up here on the shores of downtown Mill Valley, a small army of middle-aged white men floating around on life rafts of fuck-you money.

Then there's an even older layabout crowd, the ones with iron-gray hair wearing jeans and black t-shirts. Rich, famous, successful writers, musicians or whatever kind of artist. Phil Lesh, Peter Coyote, Dana Carvey and their ilk. Of course most artists, even successful ones, are broke-ass losers, but the one percent of the one percent who make it big, a lot of them end up in our toney town, like they were salmon spawned here. You think if you start selling screenplays for a million bucks a pop, or record a platinum album, you're gonna keep it real and stay in Oaktown? I'll answer the question with a question: Did Madonna stay in her East Fourth Street walk-up tenement on the Lower East Side after "Lucky Star" hit number one? You get tired of finding out your car won't start because somebody ripped out your catalytic convertor for the platinum, getting mugged by masked bandits with shotguns while you're taking your morning jog, and nowhere to buy Blue Bottle coffee. If you've got an itch to get out, and the scratch to do it, you do.

Let us not forget the trustafarians. Their grandfather invented Velcro or Sterno or whatever. They dress like bums, torn t-shirts and ripped jeans, or else eccentrically, sporting Victorian gear and top hats, killing time, waiting till the sun goes down so they can get loaded again. Believe you me, it might sound like I resent them but I don't. I want me some of that fuck-you money too so I could smoke weed all day, drink all night, and sleep till noon, although at this point I'd settle for hand-job money.

Finally, the failures. Relatively speaking, that is. They were rich once upon a time, maybe they're even still rich by normal standards, but they don't feel that way 'cause they've had the bottom drop out from under them. One-time high-fliers, they got a little too close to the sun. They might have been billionaires on paper at one time, and maybe through some sleight-of-hand accounting or a loophole that allowed quasi-legal embezzlement, they managed to make it out with a few million bucks squirreled away in the Cayman Islands. Now they spend their time riding their expensive bikes, pedaling furiously against the tide, hoping they'll eventually get back to where they think they belong and deserve to be. They meet up at the Depot after their morning ride. They'll spend the rest of the day shooting the shit and drinking coffee, yelling at stuff they read in the paper, just like the Methodonians at the Odessa back in the East Village. Libertarians one and all, they can't wait till it's legal to get blood transfusions from youngsters so they can live forever and do it all over again.

I snagged a table, piled high with garbage; the previous customers were apparently raised by servants and didn't know how to clean up after themselves. The ladies sat down while I collected the trash—coffee cups, a half-eaten sandwich, dirty napkins—and took it over to the garbage bins. But there wasn't one garbage bin there were three, a blue one, a green one and a brown one, marked "recycle," "compost" and "trash." It was like a puzzle and it took me a few moments to put the pieces together. When I returned to the table, Kirsten and Mrs. Papadopoulos had been joined by a fit guy in his mid-30s, wearing a skin-tight yellow Spandex bicyclist outfit. Our eyes met. It was the crazy guy who walloped the Mexican trucker. He spotted me, snarled, jumped to his feet and grabbed me in a tight bear hug.

Chapter 29

"Brohim! You are awesome, thanks so much for saving my bike!" Turns out he wasn't snarling—that's just his face. Resting douche face, I think the kids call it. He squeezed me tight and actually lifted me off the ground, which was no small feat.

"Oh, I see you've met my nephew Wilmer already!"

I'm not the hugging kind and was mortified by his public display of affection, but I was simultaneously relieved he wasn't smacking me upside the head with a Kryptonite lock. Ah, so this was the nephew who did something with computers and never had any trouble with the law. Cool.

Wilmer pulled away, gripping my flabby biceps tightly while he looked me over approvingly. It hurt, and I surmised he liked that. His eyes were bright and glassy; I was trying to figure out what he was on, though it might just have been a high dose of grandiosity.

"Look at you! My man! Auntie, this is the guy I told you about!"

Mrs. P scowled.

"Um, hey. I got your bike back at my house, when you wanna pick it up?"

"Nah bro, you keep it for your trouble, I already got me a new one. Mike's was having a sale, I got a tricked-out Specialized for only ten grand!" He pointed at his brand-new toy, locked up against the fence. It was sweet, all brand-new and shiny and whatnot, but I still couldn't figure out how a bicycle could cost that much. Solid gold brake calipers? Diamond-encrusted derailleurs?

"Wilmer! Leave that man alone and come sit down."

Wilmer dutifully pulled up a cast-iron chair next to hers, making an awful scraping noise on the concrete patio, and sat down. I asked the folks at the adjacent table if a vacant seat was taken, and they grimaced, like they were being forced to bite down hard on a lemon, and nodded their head, meaning yes I could take the seat but they still didn't appreciate the nerve I had for talking to them. I noisily dragged the heavy chair over to our table.

"Wilmer, can I get you anything?" Mrs. Papadopoulos asked.

"I'm good," he said, taking a swig from his CamelBak water bottle. He checked out Kirsten, quickly ogling her rack, which I had to admit was quite the eye magnet. "Hey," he said, extending a hand, assessing her like he was contemplating a hostile takeover.

"Kirsten," she said, smiling at him in a way that made me feel, well, not jealous, more like…hell yeah, it made me jealous. I was surprised because I hadn't felt much of anything toward her till now except gratitude, lust and disdain. Yet I'd have given anything right then to have had her look at me like that. Life is full of surprises. Sure, most of them suck, and this one probably did too, but hope is what keeps us going. Or at least keeps lawyers in business.

Kirsten decided this was an opportune moment to broach the matter at hand, or pre-broach it, and let me do the actual broaching. "Mrs. P, Rick has a few things he'd like to ask you about."

"Really? Him? Here, now?"

"Yeah, when's better? Besides, maybe Wilmer can help us out with some of our…questions," Kirsten said.

"Questions?" said Wilmer. "I thought we were meeting here because you had good news about the house!" Now Wilmer glared at me like he was fantasizing about smacking the white off me. His affection proved as transient and mercurial as the valley's weather.

"Yes, if you don't mind, we'd really appreciate it. Rick's trying to figure out why he was arrested." Kirsten beamed at Wilmer and put her hand on his for a second. I could see his guard dropping.

Wilmer turned back to me and smiled; I had a hunch he spent a lot of time in front of the mirror practicing. He appeared reptilian when his expression was blank, but when he grinned at you, you wanted to be his friend. "Yeah, me and you both, the man coming down. I'm out on bail myself." He punched me in the shoulder, not too hard but hard enough to hurt a little. You could tell he liked to hurt people while pretending to be friendly. What an asshole. Uh-oh—that made three. Already hit my daily quota and it wasn't even three o'clock.

I decided not to call out Mrs. P on her lie—or maybe it was news to her—about her nephew's "trouble with the law," and instead gave her my best what-do-I-have-to-do-to-get-you-in-this-house-today expression. "It would really help me out. Us out, I mean," and I angled my jaw towards Kirsten, who almost subliminally rolled her eyes.

"I don't see why not, as you're…ah…not working for me anymore," said Mrs. Papadopoulos "I hope you understand it wasn't my choice, I have no control over your company's management. Actually, I put in a good word for you."

I was taken aback. Why would she do that? I thought she loathed me. "Really? You did?"

"What the police did to you—and to me, by extension—was disgusting. *Malakas.* Not only did they arrest you for nothing, and use excessive force, they cast a pall over my sale. Tongues are wagging; they're already calling it the Taser House." What the papers would end up calling it was way worse than that, but we didn't know that yet.

"Thanks," I said, un-self-assured.

"Kirsten took over the sale while you were…indisposed. I'm very happy with her efforts so far," she said, patting Kirsten's hand. Sheesh, I thought, they're like family already. All those years Kirsten spent hanging out with the scum of the earth—bikers, drug dealers and lawyers—lying, cheating, stealing, living like an animal, working temp jobs—made her a natural realtor. She could probably convince poor Mrs. P to dump the house at a hefty discount to make a quick sale, sell it to a business partner and Kirsten would collect the commission. Then her partner would re-sell the house at full price and they'd rake it in. That's called "self-dealing," and it's illegal, but so are a lot of things folks do, but as long as you break the law with a pen instead of a gun, chances are you get away with it. There was a guy in SoCal who looked around for people who were on long-term vacations, and, working with a bent notary who gave him power of attorney, sold their houses out from under them while they were out of town. He did it for years, but eventually got caught 'cause he got greedy and did it one too many times. I think he got six months and lost his realtor's license. Anyway, after Kirsten and her partner screwed her over, the old lady would be giving Kirsten great word of mouth, telling everybody in the Redwoods what a fantastic agent she was and send her a Christmas card every year. Of course, Kirsten's partner and this nefarious plan was entirely imaginary, all this was just going on in my head. Maybe I'd ask her if she wanted to go in with me and do it, if the right moment came along. Till then, me, I was getting the short end of both sides of the stick.

"Whatever you need to ask, as long as Kirsten deems it appropriate, I'm happy to answer as best I can."

"OK, let's see, where do I start." Wilmer was giving me the stink eye. I could see he didn't want to be my bro anymore, to accompany him running the Dipsea Trail, or swimming from Alcatraz, or biking to the top of Mount Tam, all the outdoorsy stuff fit Marin bros do together. Come to think of it, I was fine with him not liking me, 'cause I sure as hell didn't want to do any of that crap either. "Remember when you had me take a peek in your attic, to see what was up there, if there was anything valuable?"

"Yes, of course." She scrunched her forehead and frowned, like she knew what was coming next. Wilmer sure looked like he did.

"While I was taking inventory, I found some...disturbing things, and I didn't tell you about it."

"Really? Why that seems totally out of character for you, Mr. Davies." She called me Mr. Davies instead of Rick for the first time since that day we first took tea together in the parlor. Or did she call me that earlier? I can't remember. She leaned back in her chair and crossed her arms.

"I thought you'd be better off not knowing about them."

"Oh, so you know what's good for me? That is rather presumptuous of you, young man."

"Yes, I realize that now, and I apologize. I was only trying to do the right thing. You see, there were some…illegal items in the dresser."

Wilmer threw his hands in the air. "Aw, he found Dad's stash!"

Chapter 30

Mrs. P looked like she was about to blow a gasket. "Wilmer! Hush up!"

"Dammit Auntie, he croaked so many years ago, and he's still haunting us!"

"We all had our difficulties with your father, but show a little respect and gratitude. You owe your success to him."

"Pfft. I don't owe him anything, I did it all myself. OK, he gave me a small stake to get me started, a measly million, but I'm the one who transformed innovation and disrupted the future first." He really said that. You can't make this stuff up. Wilmer turned to me and glared. "What did you find in that screwy attic?"

I chose my words carefully. "There was a bent spoon, some syringes, and a vial of white powder." I gave Mrs. P my best I'm-sorry-but-I-think-it's-time-we-drop-the-price face. "I thought it would be better for everybody if I just got rid of it without letting you know, I didn't want to upset you, or get mixed up with the law."

"Oh, I see. So you stole it," said Wilmer.

Now it was my turn to take fake umbrage. "How dare you, sir? I am a professional, licensed and bonded, and would never remove anything from a client's house without their express permission." My imaginary dander was up, I was almost believing my own bunkum. How dare these people imply that I was less than honest or forthcoming?

"But that's exactly what you did!"

He was right, technically. "True, but they were illegal contraband. I took them so I could dispose of them safely, without endangering my client." Here's where I laid it on thick. "I always think of the client first."

Sincerity is the key to this racket. Once you learn how to fake it, you've got it made.

Nobody said anything for a minute. Have you ever heard the expression, "an angel passed" when conversation at a lively dinner party suddenly comes to a halt? This wasn't like that. It was more like a devil passed while everybody digested my bullshit.

"OK, I'll play along. What did you do with the stuff?"

I'd stashed the Krugerrands, cash and acid in my own sock drawer, so it wasn't really like I stole them, more like I just switched hiding places, but I wasn't going to tell them that. Which reminded me, there was a Phil and Friends show coming up at the Warfield. I hadn't done acid in years, but a quarter-tab of Felix, perhaps? "I brought the spoon and the syringes over to Marin General and turned them over to an ER tech, so he could destroy them safely. Medical waste, you can't just throw it in the trash."

"The ER guy didn't say anything?"

"Nope, and neither did I, just handed it over. They see stranger stuff than that all the time, believe you me. I have a college pal who's an ER doc, he has stories."

"Gerbils? Habitrails?" said Kirsten, leaning in. A woman with a taste for human oddities. She probably liked The Stooges. Maybe even The Three Stooges. A kindred spirit.

I nodded soberly. "And it gets worse from there, you don't want to know," I said, knowing she really, really wanted to know. Truth be told, the Habitrail up the ass was the worst story he'd had, but you gotta create a little mystery if you wanna get the girl, am I right? I denied her expectations and turned back to Mrs. Papadopoulos.

"Then I did something very, very foolish—I kept the vial of white powder. I thought I—and by extension, you—could get in trouble for it. I was going to flush it down the toilet first chance I got. But what we need to know"—I glanced quickly back at Kirsten so Mrs. P and Wilmer would know who *we* meant—"is whose heroin was it? Where did it come from?" I figured now was a good time to turn the tables, put them in the hot seat, a little rope-a-dope while I got the dope on the dope.

"Wait a second, heroin? How do you know it wasn't coke?" asked Wilmer. Good question. I was wondering the same thing myself. "You just said it was a vial of white powder. Why wouldn't you think it's coke, that stuff's like a party favor around here."

"Now Wilmer," said his aunt, holding his arm. Wilmer seemed like he was about to launch himself over the little round table separating us and stab me with a fork. This guy was nuts, with poor impulse control, a violent sociopath; he had all the makings of a great CEO, politician or realtor. I had him just where I wanted him.

"Syringes, Wilmer, you know, needles. Needles are for heroin, not cocaine, everybody knows that." OK, that's not true, and I knew it. Years back, when I was living in Providence, a friend of mine was a waitress at Spats, the local watering hole. David Johansen had just played at Alumni Hall, and he and his band were hoisting a few after the show. David asked my friend, "Hey, do you mind if we take a shot glass with us? We gotta drive all the way back to New York and we wanna shoot coke so we can stay awake." Disgusted, she gave him the glass. I suppose it was polite of him to ask for it instead of just stealing it. A real gentleman.

Wilmer opened his mouth, and pointed a finger at me, seemed to think better of it, slammed his hatch shut and scowled, realizing no matter what he said it would only make it worse. I could practically see the steam coming out of his ears.

"OK, fine, heroin, if you say so. Go on."

"While I was on my way to the ER to responsibly dispose of the syringes, I made a quick stop at another client's. Like I said, the customer always comes first with me, I have a fiduciary responsibility that takes precedence even before my own personal safety."

Wilmer rolled his eyes but his aunt smiled—or maybe it was a smirk—while Kirsten gaped at me with either admiration or stunned disbelief, I couldn't tell.

"Unfortunately, it was a terrible decision. May the Good Lord forgive me." I rested my head in my hands for a moment, as if I was upset. "I was inspecting a construction site to make sure the work was not just up to code, but met the even more very stringent standards I insist upon, but while I was doing that, the general contractor apparently went into my car—"

"You didn't lock your car?" Mrs. Papadopoulos asked.

"No ma'am. I just got out for a minute or two, but it was over in Tam Valley, a sketchy neighborhood, so I should have been more careful. What I wouldn't give to get back the fifteen seconds it would have taken me to roll up my windows and lock the doors." I meant it, too. Those fifteen seconds caused me a lot of trouble. Not that it actually happened that way, but if it had, I really would have liked those fifteen seconds back. I gazed downward, like I was too ashamed to meet their gaze, then bravely looked up, as if holding back tears. Kevin Costner had nothing on me. "That contractor—that contractor was Barney, my best friend. He took your dad's dope—" I pointed an accusatory finger at Wilmer, seizing the moral high ground "—and he died because of it." I acted like I was really teed off, but was too self-restrained and professional to do anything rash about it, like I was exercising incredible self-control. "Now the cops are trying to pin Barney's death on me. What I want to know is—what was that junk doing in your attic?"

Chapter 31

Wilmer and his aunt exchanged a quick look. She took a slug of beer. Wilmer squinched and sucked his water bottle, though I'm not sure if there was any water left or if he just needed to suck on something. Kirsten was seemingly having the time of her life, calmly sipping her relaxing herbal tea, watching the drama unfold in real time. She said she wanted excitement—this had to be better than *The OC* reruns. Finally, Mrs. Papadopoulos broke what was quickly becoming another devilish silence.

"The drugs belonged to my brother-in-law. Wilmer's dad, Caleb. Caleb had various…substance abuse pro…"

"Goddamned junkie is what he was."

"Wilmer! Please!"

"No need to sugarcoat it." He swiveled to me, like I was his confessor, which is what I was, I suppose. "My old man was a big swinging…" He eyeballed his aunt. "…er, wheel back in the day. He owned apartment buildings, commercial real estate, what have you. Leveraged up the wazoo, lost it all in the crash of '87."

I remembered that. I was just out of college, had no idea what I wanted to do with myself so I was working as a temp on the trading floor of Algemene Bank Nederland. The traders pretended they had the best interests of their clients in mind while I got stoned and pretended to type on a Wang word processor. One Monday morning, as I sat at my desk, noshing on a street bagel, a ruckus broke out. The grown-ups were flipping out, screaming, "IBM is down to 48!" Then a few minutes later, "IBM is down to 42!" I watched calmly (I was already a little high) and drank my heavily sugared pushcart coffee. Whatever they were going nuts over didn't harsh my buzz—I didn't have two nickels to rub together, never mind having skin in the market. I still don't have two nickels to rub together, or skin in the market, but I do have six Krugerrands, ten grand in cash, and a sheet of acid hidden in my sock drawer, which although probably not as solid a nest egg as a diversified blue-chip stock portfolio, is much better than nothing, which is what I had when this story began. What can I tell you, I've never been a saver. I'm a good earner, grossed 200 large last year, and I spent every last cent of it—California has the world's most expensive sunshine. And in my line of work, you've got to keep up appearances. Fancy car, fancy duds, fancy alimony. Weekend trips to Napa to check out Michelin-guide starred restaurants (a bunch up there, not a one in Marin). And of course all the wine, booze, and weed. The rest of my dough, I guess I just wasted it.

Wilmer droned on, talking shit about his dad. His aunt listened stoically. Kirsten was so excited she could barely contain herself. I was weary of Wilmer's tale of woe. Realtors depend on the three Ds—divorce, death and debt—so I hear losers sing the blues all the time, and it gets nettlesome. Pro that I am, I projected empathy.

"Dad was wiped out. He took it hard, real hard. He'd been what I guess you'd call a functional alcoholic for many years. You know, 19th hole with partners and clients, three-martini lunch, that whole scene. When things went south he started hitting the sauce even harder, and suddenly he wasn't so functional anymore. My mom—Sylvia, my Aunt's sister, that's her house you're supposed to be selling now, instead of wasting my time here—she couldn't deal with it. She didn't mind that Dad was a happy drunk when he was rich, but a broke, sad drunk—she wasn't having it. She kicked him to the curb and he moved into a condo and…Auntie, are you OK with this?"

Mrs. Papadopoulos took a big gulp of her artisinal beer, no doubt savoring its toasty, biscuit-like malt flavors coasting in equilibrium with hoppy freshness, and nodded. She wore a sad expression, like she'd heard it all before, and was resigned to keep on hearing it, one way or another, for the rest of her life.

"Then he took up with a girl. For reals, a *girl*, she was a senior at Tam High. Don't look so shocked—that wouldn't fly nowadays, but it was the '80s. Roman Polanski, he went too far, but anything short of that seemed OK at the time. Anyway, this high-school bimbo introduced my Pops to cocaine. He liked it. He liked it a lot, maybe even more than he liked her. Even though he was bankrupt, and lost tens of millions, which was real money back then, he could still come up with enough lettuce for nose candy. For a few months. And when he couldn't, she dumped him like a hot potato and took up with some local rock star. Dad was—well, I don't want to say despondent, he was despondent when he started seeing her, but after he…lost her, he was crushed."

"What do you mean, 'lost her'? I thought you said she dumped him."

Wilmer and Mrs. P exchanged another one of those looks. Octavia cleared her throat and spoke. "It's a little…complicated. We didn't know what it was back then, but I guess nowadays you'd call it 'stalking.' Caleb couldn't face being alone, and he…let's just say he couldn't go back to Sylvia, not after what he'd done. You should have seen their old place in Ross—now *that* was a house! They were neighbors with Sean Penn!—before Sylvia had to move into that dump we're still trying to sell, the last holding in Caleb's real estate portfolio she'd managed to hang on to."

"OK Auntie, get to the point."

"He followed this tramp, Mary something or other, and her musician boyfriend. She quit school to go on tour with the rock star. In the spring of her senior year, can you imagine anything so silly? Moved out of her parents' house and in with the musician. But my brother-in-law was obsessed, wouldn't leave them alone. Wilmer, now it's my turn—are you OK with this?"

Wilmer swallowed hard and nodded.

"It got…very bad. There were death threats. Then, just when we thought it would never end, it all fell apart, as these things tend to do. The rock star cancelled the tour because one of his bandmates fell into a diabetic coma. Once he had nothing to do except hang around the house with that girl all day, he got sick of her soon enough. He threw her out, and her parents refused to take her back in. Turnabout is fair play, I thought at the time. Telling it now, I almost feel sorry for her. Almost. There she was, a high-school dropout, homeless, with a drug habit, a bad reputation and a stalker. And then...she disappeared."

Chapter 32

The short hairs on the back of my neck stood up. Disappeared? Had I uncovered yet another murder?

Mrs. Papadopoulos continued. "After that high school floozy suddenly vanished off the face of the earth, Caleb did too. Sylvia—we—were distraught. No cellphones back then, and he wasn't using a credit card, we had no idea where he was. Two weeks later, we get a call. The police found him in a fleabag hotel in the Tenderloin, he was…he was…"

"Dead of an overdose?"

She sighed, as if to say she wished it was that simple. "No. Naked, handcuffed to a bed, delirious, he hadn't had anything to eat or drink for days." Her voice broke. This had to be as hard for her to talk about as it was fun for me and Kirsten to hear. Wilmer took over.

"He was having withdrawals, and he literally shit the bed. And I don't mean literally the way the kids today say it—I mean he literally shit all over the bed and was laying in his own shit when they found him. What a mess. Dad was never the same after that."

I should think not.

"We brought him home, made a room for him up in the attic. Mom wouldn't let him back in her bed, but she also refused to let him become a homeless bum. I don't know if she was more concerned about the welfare of the father of her children, or her own reputation."

Kirsten shot me a sideways look—I had a feeling we both knew the answer.

"He'd already brought enough shame on the family," said Octavia. I didn't know it for a fact, but I was certain that moving Caleb to the attic, keeping him out of sight and out of mind, was her idea.

"Caleb stayed up in the attic, only going out in the middle of the night, sleeping all day. He wouldn't even come down to eat with us. Sylvia would put dinner at the bottom of the ladder every evening, but he wouldn't come down and get his food till she left. She'd find a dirty plate on the floor in the morning. From his erratic behavior and the hours he kept, we knew he was still doing drugs, but there was nothing we could do about it."

"Today they'd call that enabling," Wilmer said.

Octavia frowned at him and continued. "We didn't know where or how he was getting the stuff now that the girl was out of the picture, till we realized Caleb had some connection with her rock star boyfriend, whatever his name was, Robbs or Bobbs or something like that. We're not sure why, but we think the rock star was still supplying dope to Caleb."

Robbs? Bobbs? Dobbs. My blood froze in my veins, which made it easier to play it cool. An alarm began ringing in the back of my head as the puzzle pieces fell into place. Humans are the end product of over a billion years of evolution; our genes passed from parents to offspring over millions of generations, surviving against incredible odds by developing a powerful instinct for sensing danger. Every unconscious bullshit detector accrued over those billion years told me to *get out*. *Now*. On the other hand, what had my intuition done for me lately? It got me here, didn't it? Great. I figured I'd already sunk enough time into this mess, may as well finish up and find out what happened. I ignored my foolish instincts and kept going. Consequences, shmonsequences.

"How did you know the, uh, rock star was involved? Maybe Caleb found another source?" The rock star, I still called him. I didn't want to tattle on Dobbs. Not yet, anyway. Figures he fit into this mess; his fingerprints (and, apparently, his DNA) were splattered all over this town. Why would he supply drugs to a guy whose girlfriend he stole? After he 86'd the chippie? Then again, who knew why Dobbs did anything? Maybe he didn't know Caleb used to go with the girl. Or maybe he did, and didn't care. The better I got to know Dobbs, the less I fathomed him. Still, I was dying to learn more, in case the paradigm suddenly shifted and I'd understand him better instead of worse. I know that doesn't make any sense, but what about this whole dad-blamed story does?

"We found a pack of matches in Caleb's room," said Wilmer. "Bent backwards, making a triangle, so they could stand up. The whole row of matches still in the book, all burnt. You know, what junkies do to cook their dope. I've seen it on TV." Hadn't he just been questioning me about why I thought it was heroin? He seemed pretty sure about it now.

"I don't get it."

"The pack of matches he'd used to cook up his last shot of dope? The one that killed him? They were from the Sweetwater."

The Sweetwater. Dobbs was a silent partner. They'd closed down just a few months earlier. Coincidence? Maybe. I once heard there's no such thing as a coincidence. If that was true, there'd sure been a whole lot of nothing going on.

"Besides, Dad's death wasn't an accident."

Chapter 33

I don't think Wilmer meant to say that out loud. Didn't the family of every dead dyed-in-the-wool dope fiend say they died of an "accidental" overdose? Or if they wanted to be really high class, claim it was an "accidental overdose of pharmaceutical drugs," as if the fact that you got your shit from a shady doctor meant you weren't a lowlife? Was Wilmer about to admit that he murdered his own father, put the poison in the dope? Was this my very own Perry Mason moment? Was everything about to start finally making sense? Fat chance. I cursed myself for not having my miniature tape recorder hidden in my pocket to record his confession, like a real gumshoe. OK, I don't own a miniature tape recorder but it would have been pretty neat if I did and I'd remembered to bring it, but I probably would have forgotten it anyway.

"Wilmer, I really don't think it's anybody's…"

Wilmer cut her off. "Aw c'mon Aunt Octavia, it was 20 years ago. The truth can't hurt us now."

What did he mean? Is there a statute of limitations for murder? Like after a bunch of years they can't arrest you even if you admit you bumped off your pops? Maybe it only applied for the murder of immediate family members? Or if the victim was a total asswipe? Don't ask me, I'm just a realtor pretending to be a detective; maybe I should have asked Kirsten—she was pretending to be a realtor pretending to be a lawyer. I might have avoided a lot of trouble if I had.

"Dad was sick and tired…sick and tired of being sick and tired. He banged enough smack into his arm to kill a rhino. His hand was still on the plunger when they found him. Not such a bad way to go, I guess."

Heartbroken, outcast, broke, broken, humiliated, living in your ex's attic, committing suicide. Maybe it's just me, but I could think of better ways to go. The things people tell themselves to make it through the day.

"We never knew for sure if he meant it," said Mrs. Papadopoulos. She turned to me as if to convince herself. "The coroner ruled it a suicide, but there was no note."

"Yeah there was."

We all stopped and stared at Wilmer. "You never showed me!" said Octavia, voice quivering.

"Auntie, you didn't wanna see it. It wasn't very…nice. Dad had bad things to say about Mom, and…about us. So, screw him. I'm glad he's dead."

Mrs. Papadopoulos inhaled sharply, like she'd been stabbed in the leg with a letter opener. It was like that instant when a little kid gets hurt, they open their mouth and they go silent before they start screaming.

Ever vigilant, Kirsten piped up and saved her client, and us, from the embarrassment of an emotional outburst.

"Suicide is kind of cowardly though, don't you think? I mean, it's one thing if you've got some like, painful fatal disease or whatnot and you wanna, like, control your own destiny, but, wow, you kiss your assets goodbye and your girlfriend ditched you so you off yourself? That's hella lame." She was smart; playing dumb, making an apparent faux pas to take the focus off her client, playing the long con. Or else she was just unstable and a dunce to boot, an idiot savant who accidentally blurted out the perfect words for the moment; the jury was still out.

Wilmer looked at his aunt. "Who is she, again?"

"It told you, she's my realtor, and she's been a good friend."

"What, you've known her like two days?"

I gazed at Kirsten with newfound appreciation. Wilmer was right—Kirsten and Octavia had just met, yet Mrs. P already considered her a pal, and here she was, spilling her guts to us. Why? It didn't make any sense. I decided to change the subject before Kirsten jammed her foot in my mouth any farther. "Which brings us back to—what was the heroin still doing in the dresser drawer, all these years later?"

"Beats me," said Wilmer, shrugging. "I haven't been up in the attic since Wham was on the radio."

"Neither have I," said Mrs. Papadopoulos, "and I'm sure Sylvia hadn't either. She was quite frail these last few years. Just what are you insinuating, Mr. Davies?"

"Nothing. Just wondering if the cops will investigate when they find out where that marching powder came from." Or was it sleeping powder? Whatever.

"Investigate?"

"I'm still not sure what happened to Barney. Nobody is. Maybe he didn't know what he was into. But Barney struck me as the kind of guy who always knew what he was into, even if he didn't know what he was getting into when he started getting into it, if you catch my drift."

Something passed between Mrs. Papadopolous and Wilmer, a pre-arranged signal, perhaps. "Wilmer, I'm feeling quite tired."

"Oh, yeah, right." He raised his wrist to check the time, but he wasn't wearing a watch. "Yup, gotta go. C'mon Auntie, I'll give you a lift."

"On your bicycle?"

Wilmer glowered at me as he pulled a tiny flip phone from a hidden pocket of his skin-tight outfit. "I'll call my driver."

Two can play at this game. They wanted to drop it, I'd drop it too, even if I wasn't going to let it go. "Yeah, let's get out of here. Don't you have that thing, Kirsten?"

She picked up what I was laying down and grabbed her purse. "Thanks so much for meeting with us Octavia." Kirsten gave Mrs. Papadopoulos a quick peck on the cheek. "I'll see you Sunday at the open house, if not before. I have some clients who are *very* interested."

That cheered up the old bag. Money has a funny way of doing that for people. They get greedy. The green stuff is as much a mood-changing substance as weed, liquor, or sex, though it's not as likely to kill you. I take that back. Seems like having lots of dough makes some people loopy, they can't think straight, they're so scared of risk that they go simple and take the worst risks you can think of, like playing the market, flipping houses, or buying art in Sausalito. Don't get me wrong, I'd love to have a chance at being greedy and stupid. I had a gut feeling this case was going to end up with a windfall for me, that I was gonna end up getting what had been coming to me for a long, long time. I made a mental note to look at the new M6 on the Sonnen BMW web site, next time I had Internet access. If Kirsten could have one, why couldn't I?

We stood up and left the table before the suspects could. Then I turned around, as if I'd forgotten something. "Oh yeah, Mrs. Papadopolous, just one more thing? Who is Marjorie Khan? Why is your sister's house in her name?"

The blood drained from her face. Wilmer froze. But they recovered quickly; they were good. Too good. Wilmer took his aunt by the elbow, helping her up from the table. "Mr. Davies—sometimes, it's best not be nosy. You know what happens to nosy fellows?"

Of course I knew—duh—I'd seen *Chinatown* like eight times. So I let Wilmer whisk her away without another word, confident the truth would out.

Chapter 34

Back at Kirsten's house, we sat in our separate comfy club chairs in the home theater, watching *Six Feet Under* on DVD, snacking and drinking. I'd seen it already and it was kind of a bummer, knowing how it would turn out, but beggars can't be channel choosers.

"Something's been bothering me. When I asked Mrs. P about Marjorie Khan—she looked like she'd seen a ghost. The house is in Khan's name, at least that's what Charlie told me." We looked at the screen while we spoke; Nate Fisher was having a seizure.

Kirsten shrugged. "Who knows? If the house used to belong to Caleb Bentson, and was somehow transferred to Marjorie, there's probably all sorts of interlocking trusts and dummy corporations. Maybe Marjorie was his secretary and he made her the CEO of a fake business with a post office box in the Bahamas. That's the kind of scam my dad was into, which is why I'm in such a pickle with this house."

"Marjorie Khan owns your house too?"

She opened her mouth and, apparently thinking better, closed it and sighed. "No, I don't think so. Anyway, let it go, I doubt it means anything. Ms. Papadopolous doesn't have a devious bone in her body."

Maybe not. But Wilmer? Did he have any bones in his body that weren't devious? I meant to find out. In the meantime, we had some TV watching to do, hopefully leading to my devious bone finding its way into Kirsten's body. She was hitting the Doritos; I took care of the sauce. I was losing interest in the re-run. It had been a long day. I could barely keep my eyes open, while Kirsten was totally riveted by the show. I was about to give up all hope when she beat me to the punch.

"I'm gonna hit the hay, good night," she said. She scampered out of the room before I could say a word.

Disappointed, but not at all surprised to strike out again, at least I had the consolation prize of watching whatever I wanted. She had all the deluxe channels, so, figuring I had nothing to lose at this point, I stayed up late, drinking and watching old movies before I finally trundled off to the guest room, managed to pull off my borrowed clothes and collapsed on the bed.

I found myself in the passenger seat of my Beemer, cruising south along the Shoreline Highway. Sean had the wheel. It was my car, why was he driving? We zipped past the Muir Beach turnoff, where they had the first acid test in 1965, and turned up the hill heading towards the Green Gulch farm. Sean was driving like Neal Cassady. He was pissed. Sean, that is, not Neal. Neal's dead. Then again, so is Sean. Why was he so mad at me? I lent him my car, didn't I? But he was livid. He was complaining that my kids were running around all night, he couldn't sleep 'cause they were stomping around. I tried explaining that kids were kids, we had rugs, it wasn't my fault that there wasn't any insulation in the ceiling. Furthermore, I tried to explain that I didn't have any kids. Gail and I had flushed a couple down the drain, and that was that.

Sean wasn't having it. He sped up, recklessly skidding around hairpin turns, scaring the bejeezus out of me. It was a helluva drop if you missed one of those curves. Every few years, some drunk high school kids snuff it that way. As we rounded another bend, the outer wheels (on my side) slipped off the side of the road, spraying dust and gravel. He slammed on the brakes and we spun out, stopping mere feet from the edge of the cliff.

"Are you out of your damned mind?" I unlocked my safety belt so I could get out of the car. Sean grinned at me, grabbed the stick and threw it into reverse, gas pedal to the floor, bits of rock flying. We went over the edge. We were flying. Not really flying, dropping like a stone is more like it. The hood of the car pointed straight up into the air as we plummeted earthward. I grabbed the safety belt buckle and tried to engage it, but the gravitational pull was so intense I could barely move my arm. I inched the buckle closer to the lock, but it was like I was moving in molasses. Time slowed. The buckle was now touching the edge of the lock, and I figured I had maybe a quarter of a second to lock it in, maybe just that long to live even if I did manage to get the safety belt back on. But I had to try. I didn't want to die, not today anyway, not right now, not like this. I felt a great calm wash over me, and I said a Bardo prayer. I'm not sure if that's what it's called, but I think that's what they said on a Wayne Dyer PBS special I saw once. Time slowed down to a crawl, and I thought about all the people I had ever loved, over my whole life, realized I still loved them all, and wished them safety, health, happiness, and a life of ease. To my surprise, I thought of Gail last of all. I realized I was still in love with her too, even though I kind of hated her. At the last instant, just before we hit the ground, the belt clicked in. I didn't know if I was going to survive the crash, but at least I had tried. More importantly, I was at peace, more so than I had been in years.

Now Kirsten and I were driving along Shoreline, only this time heading in the other direction, towards Stinson Beach, in a brand-new metallic blue BMW M6 convertible. Driving the 1 by the ocean in a convertible, that's a bucket list thing, an incredible experience everybody should have at least once in their life. At least that's what the guidebooks say. It's all right, some parts by the sea are real pretty, high cliffs looming over crystal blue turquoise waters and whatnot, but if you're prone to car sickness, you'll get really car sick. Don't get me wrong, it's good. Just not as good as they say it is. Then again, what is? Anyway, we were zooming north along the coast, but this time I was driving while Kirsten rode shotgun.

We were going 100mph, but I had no trouble negotiating the winding road, like now it was my turn to be Neal Cassady. We were laughing, breeze in our hair. The arms of a white cashmere sweater were tied about my neck, Kirsten was wearing her big white Paris Hilton sunglasses. Then all of a sudden, she *was* Paris Hilton. My jailhouse dream girl. I had a huge boner.

Then, the way things happen in dreams, blackout binges, and Jim Jarmusch movies—smash cut!—and suddenly Kirsten and I were at Stinson, running in the sand barefoot. It was hot and sunny but the beach was deserted, we had it all to ourselves. I was happy to be frolicking with Kirsten but couldn't help but wonder what happened to Paris. We ran into the water, fully dressed, and the water was warm, not numbingly cold like usual. The first time I made it out to California, right after college, I went to the beach at Santa Cruz, and raced into the ocean at full speed and the cold hit me like a frickin' brick and I thought I was gonna have a heart attack and might have done if I wasn't just 21. Those beach movies I'd grown up on—lies! Say it ain't so Frankie! The Pacific Ocean is goddamn freezing! I guess the current comes down the coast from Alaska, the opposite of what happens in the Atlantic, where the warm water of the Caribbean is carried north by the gulf stream. The Pacific sure looks pretty, so blue and peaceful. Just don't try to swim in it. Or turn your back on it.

Suddenly everything was tinted dark blue, the color of night, and Kirsten and I were in the back seat of the Beemer, only it wasn't a back seat, it was a king-size bed. Now we were naked, making out. I grabbed her butt, put her left leg up over my right shoulder and pulled her close and she whispered something but I couldn't hear, so I said "What?" and she said "Stick it in, you dope!" I was just about to obey when there was a horrible banging on the car window. A cop was shining his flashlight and pounding the window with the meat of his fist, which was weird because it was a convertible and didn't have any windows. Then again, how could it have a bed for a back seat? Sometimes it's better to not ask questions, just go with the flow. I peered into the light and was blinded. And then I came like a pressure washer. How embarrassing. The damn cop wouldn't leave us alone, kept knocking, knocking, hammering on the door, saying "What the hell are you doing in there?" which I thought was silly 'cause it was pretty obvious what we were doing.

Chapter 35

Bam! Bam! Bam! The horrible racket wouldn't let up, even as I awoke. "C'mon, you lazy bastard, wake up!"

I opened my eyes; they felt glued shut. It took a few seconds for the dream to fade and for me to remember who I was. Within a few seconds I forgot most of it, except for the good part at the end. The part with Kirsten, that is, not with the cop.

"Huh? I'm awake, what's the problem?"

"It's almost noon, you can't sleep in! C'mon, he was your friend!"

I remembered. Barney's memorial was today. I'd planned on going to sleep sober last night and getting up early, but by the time it became apparent that bedtime would be a solo activity again, I'd polished off the bottle of Glenlivet. Then the Tanqueray started looking more and more appealing, till it wasn't tempting at all anymore, it just was. And then *The Big Sleep* came on TCM and what was I gonna do, not watch that? Let me give you a piece of advice. Or perhaps I should frame it as a suggestion, because I know you're thinking, why should I take unsolicited advice from this dipshit? He's been fouling up every which way but loose this whole damn story, now on top of everything else he's dumb enough to mix Glenlivet and Tanqueray. Hold your horses. I appreciate your skepticism regarding my wisdom, but all I wanted to say is: Do not, under any circumstances, mix Glenlivet and Tanqueray. Still, hard as I had tried to get blotto, I couldn't. I kept drinking and drinking but I couldn't get drunk, I just felt more and more like a chump.

"I'm up, I'm up!" I dragged myself out of the bed; it felt like I'd grown roots.

"Get a move on or we're ginna be late!"

"Yeah yeah, OK," I muttered. "Lemme take a shower."

"Good. You need one. I'm leaving some fresh underwear and socks outside the door."

Small favors were better than none. I pulled off my (or Kirsten's dad's, rather) t-shirt and boxers; it felt like I'd been wearing them for two months, not two days. I hit the shower. I guzzled water straight out the incredibly expensive shower head. The gentle rain felt like a hundred tiny hammers smashing my head. I liked being in the marble cubicle—isolated, safe, cut off from the world, so I stayed in a long time, even though I didn't whack off. I didn't have to, after last night's spectacular wet dream, the first I'd had in decades. I just didn't want to rejoin reality, or what passes for it in these parts. Eventually I had to. I let myself drip-dry; even Kirsten's 1000-thread-count soft Egyptian towels would have felt like sandpaper in my condition. I reached in the medicine cabinet and chewed three aspirin. Once again I missed my little purple friends.

I slipped my safari suit back on. I had taken a shine to it. I padded over to the living room where Kirsten was waiting, tapping her foot. She was wearing her white Chanel suit again, which I now realized was the real deal, not a cheap copy. She looked like a million bucks, or maybe ten million, what with inflation. Ah, what am I talking about—she'd have looked good in a potato sack.

"About time."

"Yeah yeah, I'm sorry, c'mon let's go."

"For fuck's sake, he was your friend, the least you could do is be on time, after you killed him."

"Hey, you're the one who insisted we go. I hate memorials, they remind me of other memorials and make me feel bad, you know?"

"Yeah, God forbid you should have a feeling. Anyway, this is not just a social call. We might be able to figure out who poisoned Barney by seeing who's at the service. The murderers always show up."

"Right, to see the result of their handiwork, I get that."

We got in her Hummer—Barney hated environmentalists and regulations, they mucked up his work, so it was in his honor—and got on the 101 north. I stared out the window, wondering if Baron Davis would re-sign with the Warriors. I wouldn't blame him if he left. Who doesn't want to be appreciated? Blockhead Donnie Nelson, not playing Baron in the second half. We passed Lucky Drive and the train trestle where Clint Eastwood shot Andrew Robinson at the end of *Dirty Harry* and continued towards San Rafael. We passed the Richmond Bridge turnoff, the car dealerships and then the Civic Center and the county jail. The jail may have been designed by a world-famous architect, and looks much better from the outside, but it still made me nervous. Now and forevermore I'd think of it as where I spent the day in stir, rather than a one-minute walk from where they recorded *Frampton Comes Alive*. Can you have PTSD from something that happened just two days ago? Maybe not but it still gave me the heebie-jeebies. We exited at Lucas Valley and rumbled through serpentine side streets up a steep slope till we made it to the top of the hill and the Unitarian Church.

The church was shaped like a giant ark. There aren't that many religious people around these parts. I think it was Dick Gregory who said there are more dogs than Christians in Marin. Cathedrals have been replaced by cathedral ceilings, so folks can worship themselves and their prosperity in the comfort and privacy of their own home. What churches we do have are greatly outnumbered by European automotive repair shops, acupuncture clinics and cat hospitals.

The Unitarians keep a low profile and are all right by me. They don't seem to bother anybody; they're not even God botherers. I'm not sure if they even pray to God, or else if they just believe in The Force, or maybe are just dedicated to acting pleasant to everybody in a non-denominational way, and hosting pot luck dinners.

I spied Dobbs' red Ferrari in the parking lot. I put the battery back in my Treo, set the time, and placed it under the Ferrari's rear wheel.

"What are you doing?" Kirsten asked.

"You'll see. Cool trick I picked up from an old detective flick." She tried to raise an eyebrow and was about to say something, but held her tongue.

Chapter 36

We entered the vast nave. The joint was jumping. Barney had a lot of friends. Or at least a lot of acquaintances. For all I know they could have been disgruntled ex-clients (are there any other kind, in the construction business?) who'd shown up to gloat. Massive timbers stretched over our heads, holding up the ceiling like an upside-down ship's hull. I wondered what would happen if there was a big earthquake. It would probably end up as a clipping on Hannibal Lecter's cell wall. If he was real. But how much of any of this was real? At the front of the hall, the sanctuary was flanked by two massive portraits. I'm pretty sure both paintings were supposed to be representations of Jesus, but the one on the left looked like Charlie Manson and the one on the right like a blond stoner surf dude.

I spotted Dobbs in the rear pew, sporting a ratty green t-shirt and ripped, dirty cargo shorts. His graying beard got bigger every time I saw him. They say the bees are dying out. Maybe it's because they get confused and try to live in Dobbs' beard. He was starting to resemble a crazed mullah, a member of a ZZ Top tribute band, or a web developer from Williamsburg. Another contestant on *Homeless or Mill Valley Millionaire*—you make the call! Kirsten and I sat down next to him. The pews had cushions and foot rests and were quite comfortable, as far as these things go. Unitarians are not into self-flagellation. We shook hands, and he smiled at Kirsten in a way I did not appreciate. There was a hole in the front of his t-shirt the size of a half dollar and his left nipple poked out of it.

At the altar stood a whip-thin elderly man with a long white beard, in a flowing white robe, playing guitar. He wore leather sandals, the kind you see in '50s Bible movies. He was belting out an old Dylan tune, or what sounded like a mashup of old Dylan songs; the acoustics of the church were wonderful, but he was trying to imitate Dylan and missed the whole point and just mumbled and groaned, without proper phrasing or intonation, so I could barely make out a word, though I thought I heard "wind," "chimes" and "freedom." Come to think of it, he kind of hit the nail on the head. The congregation sang along half-heartedly, like they were embarrassed. I sure was.

The song wound down, not really ending so much as petering out, followed by light applause, almost a golf clap. "Thank you everybody. As you all know, Barney was a beloved man who touched many hearts. One of his dear friends wanted to be here, but couldn't make the long trip. But thanks to technology, he can be here now. Please give me a moment while I get the computer hooked up to the projectors here." He began fiddling with some electronic equipment. A couple of gray-headed hippie ladies wearing white muslin dresses went up to help him.

The gizmos they're coming up with these days, boy howdy. When I was a kid, they said in the 21st century we'd have vacations on the moon, jetpacks and visual phones. We got the phones at least. Then again, they also predicted a dystopian police state, environmental disaster and constant cyber surveillance, so I guess we got more than half of what we were promised.

The projector turned on and an image of a frail senior, who looked like he'd forgotten to shave for a couple of weeks, filled the ten-foot-tall screen. "Ladies and gentlemen, please give a warm welcome to a good friend of Barney, joining us here from the Big Island, the one and only Ram Dass."

I whispered to Kirsten, "Hey, you know what's funny? He's gay, right? And his name is Rammed Ass."

Kirsten punched me in the arm and whisper yelled, "What are you, twelve?"

The apparition on the screen began to speak, with some difficulty, like he'd had a stroke or two. "Thank you Rabbi Marvin."

I turned to Dobbs. "I didn't know Barney was Jewish." There are Jews in Marin but, like the Unitarians, they keep it on the DL, and are more likely to buy a Christmas tree than matzoh.

Dobbs shrugged. "He wasn't, but we couldn't get Thich Nhat Hahn on such short notice, and we figured the singing rabbi was our next best bet."

Rabbi Marvin asked Ram Dass how his Jewish faith helped him deal with tragedies like what befell Barney. Ram Dass looked up, in deep contemplation. Finally, he spoke. "Well, it didn't hurt." The audience burst into laughter.

Ram Dass rambled on, telling us how he was swimming in a warm bath of love and light. Yup, sounded like Hawaii, or the idealized version of it anyway, which I guess you get to experience if you're rich enough. Finally, Rabbi Marvin thanked him and turned off the computer. Then he performed a West African folk dance. The old hippie ladies joined him onstage and swayed and shimmied to the music like they were on Orange Sunshine at a Moby Grape concert. I don't know much about Jewish funerals, but this one didn't seem especially traditional. Wasn't somebody supposed to step on a glass or something?

I sat there soaking in the sad spectacle. I found myself reflecting over my entire life, reviewing it year by year, gig by gig, lover by lover, the way you do at funerals, and realized that everything I'd ever done, from childhood to adolescence to adulthood, the entire spectrum of my existence, had all lead me to this excruciating moment. Watching the graying, chunky, bourgeois Bohemian women dance, I was pretty sure this was the low point not only of the service, but of my whole life. Turns out I was wrong. Again. It was starting to become an annoying habit. But like a degenerate gambler with no understanding of statistics, I figured that the odds were finally starting to turn in my favor so I kept doubling down and tossing the dice, again and again, even though I knew they were loaded.

Rabbi Marvin began playing a battered old harmonium, singing some kind of Hare Krishna chant, but he kept pausing, apparently forgetting how it went, and the captive audience trying to sing along had to stop and wait for him to remember. It was brutal.

Dobbs poked me in the ribs with an elbow. "Hey," he said, probably too loud, "you see this?" and handed me a *Marin IJ*. It was a couple of days old. My eyes widened as I read the headline.

> **Second Woman Found Dead By Trailside**
> Mt. Tamalpais - A search team of police, firemen and EMTs discovered the body of Ms. Marjorie Khan, née Marjorie Hart, of New York City. Ms. Khan was last seen Wednesday morning by her father, with whom she had lunch, before going to Marin for "hiking and to see an old friend." Ms. Khan grew up in Mill Valley, and attended Tam High, but left Marin shortly before graduating and has lived in New York since 1987. Foul play has not been ruled out."

"This is the girl they found the other day, right? That makes like two in two weeks, right? Now keep reading, it gets really weird." He grinned; Dobbs loves weird stuff.

I looked back at the paper.

> "Ms. Khan married local real estate mogul Caleb Bentson in 1986, in a ceremony performed by Hugh Romney. They separated

shortly thereafter, just before Mr. Bentson's untimely death. While in New York she married a partner at her law firm, John Kahn."

Chapter 37

Why was Dobbs showing this to me, here, now? Was he trying to get a rise out of me? Did he know I was on to him? Or was he trying to throw me off his trail? Now was the time to put my cards on the table. They were lousy cards, but they were all I had. Come to daddy, on an inside straight.

"Dobbs, didn't you used to go with her?"

"Who?"

I stabbed the paper with a finger. "Her. Marjorie Khan. Or Marjorie Bentson. Or whatever her name was at the time."

He shrugged. "Maybe. Who knows? I don't remember the '80s so good."

On this I did not doubt him. I'd known Dobbs for ages, but did I really know him? Who was this guy? Was the whole acid-casualty routine just a front? Was Dobbs secretly a diabolical killer as well as a spaced-out rock star? He'd gotten Barney's memorial set up fast—too fast, maybe. Had he booked the room in advance, knowing he'd need it? Was his famous thousand-yard stare and black-hole eyes a result of too many drugs—or too many murders? It added up—he killed Wilmer's dad with bad junk out of jealousy, and he scared Marjorie off to New York, then he killed Marjorie when she returned to town, because she knew the truth. And then he tried to kill me by cutting the brake lines on my car, but got dopey old Sean instead.

On the other hand, maybe Dobbs was innocent, and it was Wilmer who killed his dad, back when he was a psycho teenager, before he was a psycho adult, and then he killed Marjorie when she came back to town. I knew Marjorie was listed as the house's owner, probably one of those funky deals where Caleb's ex Sylvia got a life estate, was able to stay there as long as she lived, and Marjorie couldn't sell it till Sylvia died. That's why Sylvia let the house go to hell—why add value to the property of someone you hate? Or maybe it was Octavia who had Wilmer act as her gunsel and knock off Marjorie, so the house would go back to her. Wilmer was sure violent enough to do it. And Octavia would let him use the moolah from the sale to keep his startup solvent.

On the other hand, maybe it was something else, maybe something so close and obvious I couldn't see it. I'd cross that bridge when I came to it. I needed more clues, had to gather more evidence, keep digging. I re-read the article. I wanted to ask Dobbs more questions but when I looked up he was gone; he'd taken a powder, given me the slip. Or maybe he was as bored as I was and just left.

The excruciating service ended shortly thereafter, praise the lord. It was as painful as a '95 Dead show, not because the ceremony reminded me of previous losses I've suffered, or because Rabbi Marvin's voice sounded like a choking frog, or even because I'd miss Barney that much. I mean, he was a nice enough guy, even if I only trusted him about half as far as I could throw him, but that's pretty good for a contractor. Seriously, what other business has such a low barrier to entry? Anybody who knows how to swing a hammer or slap a paintbrush around can get some business cards printed up at Kinko's and call himself a contractor. You need to get some kind of license—but Harvard Business School it ain't. Then you just cruise over to the Home Depot and pick up a crew of illegal workers for the day, do that a few times till you find some guys you like—it helps to know a little Mexican—and off you go. Sometimes you have to pull a permit, but usually, especially if it's in the county and not Mill Valley proper, you can get away with murder. Virtual strangers, who heard about you by word of mouth, will hand over fatty boombah advance checks and the keys to their house, no questions asked. You could be a paroled killer fresh out of the slammer—and who the hell knows what the undocumented workers are running from back in El Salvador or Nicaragua or wherever. It's a sketchy business. But I could trust Barney to rip me off at an acceptable rate. There was a lot to be said for that. We'd worked on a half-dozen houses over the last few years and had banked major coin. I wished I'd manage to save some of it. Where it all went, I don't know. Probably the same place Barney went. Anyway, I'd miss him, at least till I found a replacement, but no, I was hardly broken up by his death. Better him than me, you know what I'm saying?

No, it wasn't Barney's untimely demise that upset me, nor was it the outpouring of raw emotion from at least a few of the attendees. It was just plain dull: the bad music with the gobbledygook lyrics, bad dancing, and one self-congratulatory ho-hum humdrum eulogy after another. I had a headache. I let my head hang low. I needed a pick-me-up, and pronto.

"Hey, are you OK?" Kirsten asked, reading me wrong. She put a hand on my shoulder and rubbed. I liked that.

"Yeah, I'm all right." My incipient tears were from the pain of my hangover, but she didn't need to know that. "Can we go?"

"It's OK, it's over. Let's pay our respects."

Luckily, Barney wasn't married and didn't have any kids, so paying our respects entailed waving hello from across the room to some people I vaguely knew, cruising around the hors d'oeuvres table and scarfing down a few quick plastic cups of cheap wine. We didn't stay long; the rotgut wasn't good enough to hang out for, but it did take the edge off.

Back in the parking lot, no surprise, Dobbs' Ferrari was gone. I walked over to where it had been parked and found my Treo. The screen was cracked and it wouldn't turn on. I was hoping that I'd be able to see what time Dobbs left, that the phone's clock would stop working and show the exact time he ran over it. I guess I don't know much about cellphones. I didn't know when Dobbs had left, but I did know what time it was now: time for an iPhone! How could Verizon doubt the phone had been in a car crash now?

Kirsten stood there arms akimbo, smirking. "How'd that work out for you?" I frowned sheepishly. A few minutes later we were barreling back south on the 101.

"Enough dilly-dallying, Rick. It's time to get to the bottom of this."

"Absolutely. What do you have in mind?"

"Let's head back to Mill Valium. I've got an idea. We're ginna consult a cat psychic."

"Come again?"

Chapter 38

"You being a guy and all, I bet you didn't notice that Mrs. P's dead sister had a cat. Lots of cats."

"Are you kidding? Me and Mr. Frank go back. Took an awful lot of scrubbing to get his smell out."

"I think we should ask him some questions."

"Excuse me?"

"Do you believe in psychic phenomena?"

"Like what, ESP? Déjà vu?"

"More like vibrations, ripples in the fabric of reality. Morphogenic fields."

"Um, yeah, sure. Why not? I believe in Yetis, the chupacabra and Bat Boy. It's fun!" Sounded like she'd been hanging out with Dobbs.

"No man, not like that, like, y'know, the multiverse. Vibrations emanating from alternate timelines. And it's not just people who give off these vibrations—animals do too."

There were plenty of New Agers in Marin—hell, we'd just escaped from a whole nest of them—but Kirsten sounded like she ran a crystal shop in Sedona for aliens from the hollow Earth. I'd heard some of those AA people got into all sorts of weird spiritual shit—Hinduism, meditation, Pilates. I guess Jesus wasn't spooky enough for them, or maybe he was just old hat.

"Uh, just what is it you're suggesting?"

"If something bad, like, really bad, happened in that house, Mr. Frank would know about it. Not maybe in so many words, but more like images of the bad sensations. A cat psychic could interpret them for us."

"Fine with me, just let me check with my secretary first to make sure my schedule is clear." I pressed my fingers to my temples, shut my eyes and chanted "Ommmmmm…ommmmmmmm…ommmmmmmmm." I opened my eyes. "Yeah, I'm good, let's go."

Kirsten tried to glower but her face wasn't having it. "You slay me. We'll get you signed up at the Monday night open mike at the Sweetwater."

The Sweetwater. Again. I let it drop and decided to play along. See a cat psychic. Why not? What would it cost me? And we'd probably get more cogent information from some stiff's semi-feral kitty than Dobbs.

We got off at the Tam Valley exit, drove past the burned-down hotel that was built on an Indian burial ground and took our lives in our hands by taking a left onto Tennessee Valley Road. They really ought to have a stoplight there, the traffic can't get any worse than it is already. "Where we going? Does the cat psychic have an office here?"

"No, she lives in Denver. But she's not available on Saturdays till later in the afternoon."

"Seriously? You get psychic readings for a cat over the phone?"

"Make fun all you want. But my friend Jerylynn, her cat Monty was missing for two days? She called the cat psychic, and she told Jerylynn to imagine Monty enveloped in a purple bubble and to call his name. See, the psychic figured out Monty was jealous of Marmie, Jerylynn's new cat, and that she had to treat Monty as the alpha cat in the house so he'd feel comfortable. And it worked!"

"That's an amazing story," I said as we pulled into a dirt parking lot. "So Monty came home?"

"Nah, they found him out back. He'd been killed by a coyote. But they never would have known he was there if not for the psychic."

OK. "So where are we going now?"

"I thought we should go for a hike while we wait. This is the Tennessee Beach trailhead. Some exercise will do us some good. And by us, I mean you."

When I was younger and lived in New York City, the most dreaded words in the English language were "Will you come see my band?" In Marin it's "Let's go for a hike," especially if you're like me, an out-of-shape city slicker who doesn't get the appeal of trudging around the woods for no reason for an hour or two and then wasting another hour or two slogging back. Sure you see some pretty stuff, but I can see pretty stuff out my car window and I don't get all sweaty and there's no risk of Lyme disease.

I didn't say anything but she knew me well enough by now that I didn't have to. "C'mon, don't be a wuss. Sweat out some of that alcohol. How long have you lived in Mill Valley now?"

"Twelve years."

"And you haven't been to Tennessee Beach yet? I mean, it's not even a hike, it's mostly flat. Five-year-olds can handle it."

"Yeah, cause they don't know any better."

She didn't say anything, just waited.

"Oh all right." I gave in pretty easy, didn't I? But really, what choice did I have? Ever since she'd sprung me from the big house, I'd practically been Kirsten's captive. Not for the first time, I wondered why she was taking care of me like this. First it seemed she wanted me as her sex slave, and I was good with that, but besides that first roll in the hay she'd been cold as a July day in the Sunset. No more nookie, but she supplied me with top-shelf hooch and let me watch TV on her giant set and chillax at her luxurious crib, so I didn't complain. But what did she *really* want from me? She claimed she was just looking for action, but while Diet Coke and Doritos (for her; liquor and limes for me) and binge watching *America's Next Top Model* was my kind of night off-the-town, it wasn't exactly high drama. It was almost as if she had me under house arrest.

It was Saturday so the unpaved parking lot was crowded, plenty of folks coming up from the city, dozens of cars lined up willy-nilly. Kirsten squeezed her big-ass Hummer between a Highlander and a Pilot, both with giant iron bike racks sticking out the back. I could barely open my door enough to wriggle out. I had a bad feeling about this. I was sure if the Highlander or Pilot owners had kids with them—and why else would you own a car like that?—we'd come back to find big dents in Kirsten's car doors.

Chapter 39

I had to admit, once I overcame a couple dozen years of inertia and got moving, the hike was lovely. The air was crisp, clean and aromatic. My favorite part about Marin is the air, a mixture of Pacific ocean and eucalyptus. Clean. My New York lungs quit squeaking a year after I moved out here, and I stopped getting bronchitis every winter. It's almost enough to make you forget about the tech bros, frat boys and bankers who've forced out the old hippies and artists and weirdos (except for the rich weirdos) and run amok, tearing down every old bungalow and putting up 4500-square-foot McMansions in their place. But who am I to judge my bread and butter?

Kirsten led me down a wide, gently sloping gravel path. As far as hikes went, it wasn't half bad, not much worse than strolling about town. It was crowded: families with little kids, hipsters from the city, retired couples. An incredibly diverse display of just about every kind of affluent white person you could imagine. The tots were doing fine, so I didn't gripe, although I wanted to, but I'd already shamed myself enough in Kirsten's eyes to last a lifetime. Forty-five minutes later, we finally made it to Tennessee Beach. It was gorgeous. Cerulean blue waters and tidal pools, condors or whatever the hell kind of giant birds they were flying overhead. Folks took off their shoes, rolled up their pants and frolicked in the shallow water. I finally understood what Jerry meant when he said there ain't no place he'd rather be, so the trip was worth it for that.

"OK, it's spectacular," I said. "Can we leave now? And maybe stop over at the 2am Club for a minute? We could play pool." And I could have a much-needed eye opener.

"Sure," she said, surprising me. "I like playing pool, and the Deuce is the cleanest dive bar I've ever been in." She gazed out at the water, smoking a cigarette.

"You know Jack Kerouac lived on the roof of the Deuce for a few months in the summer of '47?"

"Who? Huey Lewis did his album cover there, that's all I know."

Her cigarette smelled good. "Gimme one a those bad boys."

She passed me her smoke and lit another. We puffed in silence and watched the waves. She stubbed out her butt and said, "All right you giant baby, let's go. We'll take a shortcut back." Sounded good to me. I never met a shortcut I didn't like.

Kirsten headed up the hill but turned left onto a different trail, narrower and more rugged-looking than the one that brought us here. This one ran parallel to the beach. She quickly scrambled up the path like a mountain goat. I followed carefully, still smoking. Kirsten's dad's white patent-leather shoes had been fine on the first, almost-level path, but now I was slipping on the scree, having trouble keeping my footing. This was more like what I thought of as hiking. It sucked major ass. I was gasping and wheezing like the little engine who couldn't. I probably should have put out my cigarette but it was only halfway done and I hadn't smoked in so long, other than the past couple of days, that I wanted the whole enchilada.

"Are you sure we're going the right way?"

She didn't turn around so half her words were lost in the wind. "Have…given you…before?"

Unlike the crowded main pathway we'd taken to get to the ocean, this one was deserted. I could see why. It was getting ever steeper, littered with boulders big and small so it was hard to figure where to plant your feet. I wasn't sure it was even a path. Now I couldn't hear anybody back at the beach anymore, but I could still see the water. We had the place to ourselves. Alone at last. Just like my dream, except now I was out of breath, sweaty and tired from climbing instead of boning.

Suddenly, it felt like a grenade went off inside my skull. I screamed and crumbled to the ground. As I was falling, my thoughts went into hyper-speed. All at once it was obvious who the trailside killer was. The bright sunshine dimmed and it all went black.

Chapter 40

I hovered in midair, prone, and gazed down at my supine body. I felt very calm floating a few feet above myself. From this perspective, I didn't seem like such a bad guy. Sure, I'd pulled some major boners. Who hasn't? I peeped sideways and saw a beautiful blonde hanging in the air next to me. She reminded me of that green chick from *Lost In Space*, only she wasn't green, except for her eyes, which were green flecked with starry shards of copper. She beamed at me.

"Do you want to come with me?" she asked. It was an enticing offer. I had a big decision to make. I was tempted to just drift away with her, forget about this rotten world and all of its cockamamie problems—spoiled teenagers, crooked contractors, Lexus drivers, jackasses in giant pick-up trucks parking in the compact-only spaces at the Town Center, nettlesome neighbors, loser landlords, bitchy bosses and unrequited love—but I still had business to take care of. There was that upcoming Phil & Friends show, I had to finish my science fiction novel, and I still hadn't picked up a lint brush from Bed, Bath & Beyond. I closed my eyes and slowly sank back down and became one with myself again.

I came to and found myself in a white room—white walls, white curtains. A man and a woman, both dressed in white, stood over me. Was I in heaven? No such luck. More the closest you can get to its opposite here on Earth—I was in a hospital.

The nurse said to the doctor—or maybe it was the other way around, it's hard to tell these days—"He's waking up."

Last thing I remembered, it felt like a mule had kicked me upside the head, and I figured I was a goner. Kirsten had lured me out to the boonies to bump me off, just like she'd iced Marjorie Khan. The first woman killed on the Tam trail a few weeks earlier, the Tantric Yoga teacher, was also probably an old flame of Caleb's. Or maybe another of Dobbs' discarded groupies. Or maybe just a diversion to throw me off track. My latest theory: Kirsten was the old lady's niece and Wilmer's sister, she killed Marjorie to avenge her dad. Or maybe, maybe Kirsten had murdered her dad 20 years ago by poisoning his smack, and Marjorie knew it, and once she came back, there was only one way to keep her mum. Or maybe she did it just so she and her family got to keep the house, and the profits, when I sold it for them. Octavia had played it cool, not tipping me to their relationship, but when I started at the end and worked backwards it was obvious. I stumbled right into the middle of it, and Kirsten had to send me to the boneyard so I wouldn't squawk. Murder's like potato chips—once you start, it's hard to stop.

"What happened?" I asked the doctor, or nurse, or janitor, or whatever he was.

"I'm afraid you had a heart attack, Mr. Davies."

"What? What about my head? Who clipped me?"

He consulted his clipboard. Yeah, docs still used pen and paper in those days, can you believe it? The iPad was still like three years away. It was the dark ages and we didn't even realize it. It's hard for the kids today to imagine how rough we had it in 2008—you wanted Netflix you had to wait for the mail, there was no WiFi on airplanes, and phones were for talking. Now that I think about it, everything was better back then.

"Er, no, your head's fine. You're terribly out of shape and had a myocardial infarction. Do you drink? Smoke?"

"Yes. No. I mean, I have a cocktail from time to time, but no, I don't smoke. Well, actually, I took up smoking again recently."

"Bad idea. Cut down on the booze, quit the cigarettes, start exercising, lose some weight and you might collect Social Security some day."

That was a pretty tall order; I didn't think I could do it all at once.

"Yeah, I could stand to lose 20 pounds."

"Try 40," said the doc. "You've got high cholesterol and high blood pressure. You're a ticking time bomb. Thank your lucky stars you weren't alone."

"Kirsten?" My eyes narrowed. Didn't they know she tried to kill me, that she was a homicidal maniac?

"You owe her your life, Mr. Davies. It was only through her quick thinking that we managed to get a helicopter out to you in time. A few more minutes and you wouldn't have made it."

I wasn't buying it. If Kirsten didn't rub out the old man, who had poisoned the dope that killed Barney? Who offed the girls on the trail? And who did in Sean? I almost forgot about him. Just when I thought I had it all sussed out, I was more confused than ever.

"Where is she? I'd like to talk to her."

"And she'd like to talk to you. I'll send her in." The doc and the nurse left the room and Kirsten entered, accompanied by my two detective pals, Keyes and that simian mouth-breather McGee. My head was still foggy and I thought they had her under arrest, and as a courtesy escorted her to my room so she could confess. Or maybe just apologize for trying to whack me.

Kirsten approached my bedside, put a hand on my shoulder and smiled at me, smiled at me like I'd been waiting for her to smile at me since I first laid eyes on her, none of this upside-down frowny Botox grimace I'd been getting up till now.

"Hey Rick, how you doing?"

I know, it sounds crazy, but even after she tried to terminate me with extreme prejudice, I don't think I've ever been happier to see anybody in my life. I realized what I'd known deep inside since the moment I'd met her—Kirsten was my soul mate. Two natural-born salesmen, we were made for each other, and she felt it too, I could tell by the way she was looking at me. I reached up to take hold of her hand. Cold steel bit into my wrist as the handcuffs shackling me to the hospital bed held me back.

"What the hell?" I shot daggers at the detectives. "Officers, what's the meaning of this?"

"I'm afraid you're under arrest, Mr. Davies," said Detective Keyes. McGee grinned.

"What? That's nuts! I didn't put poison in the junk! And if Kirsten didn't, then Wilmer or Mrs. P did!"

"There wasn't any poison."

"Huh?"

"Nobody poisoned Barney. We just got back from the crime lab," said Keyes. "Turns out, that vial of white powder you gave Barney? It was Mannitol. Baby laxative. What they use to cut cocaine."

"But what about his discolored fingernails? Doesn't that mean arsenic?"

"Could do, but not in this case. He was clumsy with a hammer."

"Then what killed him?"

Kirsten piped in. "That heavy dresser you asked him to move? It was too much for his heart. Simple as that."

"So Sylvia didn't poison her husband? She's not your mom? You didn't kill your old man and his girlfriends? Dobbs didn't help you out? Octavia and Wilmer didn't kill Marjorie Khan? Charlie didn't set me up by putting my business card in Marjorie Khan's pocket?"

Kirsten seemed concerned. She turned to the two detectives. "I think he's delirious. You guys read him his rights already, right?"

Detective Keyes said, "Yeah, he's been in and out for a couple of hours, he probably doesn't remember, but good enough for government work."

Kirsten nodded and looked back down at me. "Look, Octavia's a sweet old lady, and her sister was probably nice too. The husband, Caleb, he was a dirtbag, and he OD'd. No mystery. It's no wonder you found a secret stash in his old dresser. But you really shouldn't have taken the Krugerrands and the cash. Octavia put them there. She was testing you to see if you were an honest realtor, if she could trust you with the sale of the house."

"That's nuts! Since when did honesty have anything to do with being a good realtor?"

She shrugged. "Good point. But that's the story—the old lady planted valuables up there, and when you didn't give them to her, she hired me to tail you." Kirsten fished a card out of her purse and flashed it at me. It had a picture of a magnifying glass, with a drawing of an eye inside it. It had her name on it, then California Association of Licensed Investigators. Copperplate, embossed. Thick, glossy stock. Classy.

"These gentlemen busted you for grand theft at the open house, but they tased you, so you don't remember. But they nabbed you too soon, didn't have enough evidence to hold you so they turned you loose. I kept you on ice while we were waiting to get a warrant to search your house. We found the gold, and the ten grand in cash. Well, $9800—dude, that was idiotic to give her the hundreds from her own roll—they were marked. Once we were able to match the bills you gave Mrs. P to the ones you had in your drawer, it was all over. We just had to wait till that was confirmed. Why else do you think I would take you into my home like that?"

"Cause you had a crush on me? Cause you were bored? That's what you said!"

She shrugged. "It's the truth, kind of. My parents left me a boatload of green and I travelled around the world a couple of times and then laid around the house for a year and yeah, I was bored out of my skull, so I became a PI. It gives me structure. But this one was personal too."

"I knew it! Caleb Bentson *was* your dad! Or maybe Octavia's your mom and he was your uncle!"

"Oh man! Let it go already. No, it was because of Barney. We were tight. He had almost a year, he was doing great before you came along."

"A year? A year of what?"

She rolled her eyes. "Never mind."

"Wait, what about the first woman who was murdered on the trail, the Yoga teacher? And what about Marjorie Khan?"

"Two completely unrelated accidents. Slip and falls. Coincidence. People die all the time. These things happen."

"But...somebody was trying to kill me because I was getting too close to the truth! They cut the brake cables on my car and Sean got killed instead of me! What about that?"

Keyes broke in. "Oh yeah, thanks for reminding me. Sean had a high level of morphine sulfate in his blood at the time of his death. He nodded out at the wheel and went off the cliff. We found a prescription bottle at the scene. A prescription that didn't belong to you, Mr. Davies. Sorry to inform you, but besides the original grand larceny beef, we're also charging you with involuntary manslaughter." He gave me a toothy, tobacco-stained grin. He didn't seem sorry at all.

Somehow it wasn't sinking in. I was desperate, grasping at straws. "What about the cat psychic? What did Mr. Frank say?"

McGee chuckled. "We couldn't get a word out of him. Maybe his lawyer got to him first and had him clam up. It was a regular cat-tastrophe." Keyes and McGee threw their heads back and laughed uproariously; I half-expected a freeze frame.

Kirsten raised her shoulders, palms up, as if to say, "What can I tell you?"

I finally realized why I couldn't crack this case. The guy I was hunting was too close. Sitting at the same desk as I was. The trail of clues led right back to yours truly.

"Wait, one last thing. Just tell me the truth—you never felt anything for me?"

Kirsten leaned over, patted my chest, and pecked my cheek. I peeked down her dress one last time. "Of course I did. Hey, in another life...but not in this one. I've spent too much time with bad boys already, and there's no way I'm letting the killer inside me. Not more than once anyway." She smiled again, turned, and walked away. I'd heard about a gal kissing a guy and stabbing him in the back at the same time, but I never thought it would happen to me. Keyes and McGee stayed behind.

"You'll wait for me, right?" I shouted after her as she left the room. She didn't look back.

I closed my eyes, focused, concentrated as hard as I could and tried to will my soul to rise out of my body again, to float back up to the ceiling and fly away with the blonde angel.

It didn't work.

ACKNOWLEDGEMENTS

This book wouldn't have happened without Maggie Estep. She was working as a real estate agent in the Hudson Valley, and we were chatting online and she told me about a new estate sale, how when she'd first gone to the house and went up to the attic it was creepy as hell, full of weird old stuff. So I said, "Hey, you should write a mystery novel about a realtor who stumbles onto an old murder case after looking in a scary old attic."

"That's a great idea!" she said, "Let's write it together!"

And a week later she was gone.

So I decided to write it myself. And here it is. Thank you Maggie, it wouldn't have happened without you. I miss you.

I'd also like to send a big thank you and much love to all of my early readers for their notes, corrections and encouragement: Luciann Meisler, Jenny Wade, Margo West, Peter Blauner, Drew Hubner, Kenneth Wishnia, Mark Netter, Patrick O'Neil, Fred Weiler, "Jerylynn," and J. Macon King.

And of course, the Sensitive Skin crew, for all they do...

Also available from **Sensitive Skin:**

Mayakovsky Maximum Access
selected poems by Vladimir Mayakovsky
translated with commentary by Jenny Wade

"Jenny Wade's superb translations of the poems of Vladimir Mayakovsky, her enchanting comments and brief essays on the very poems of the first street poet of the last century, help to end the crime that, to this day, only a portion of his immense written and visual works have been published in the United States. Mayakovsky is the real and realist father of the American Beat Generation. Jenny Wade's translations make that actuality emphatic."
—Jack Hirschman, Poet Laureate Emeritus of San Francisco

The Last Poet of the Village
selected poems by Sergei Yesenin
translated with commentary by Anton Yakovlev

"Yakovlev has given us something I thought impossible, an English Yesenin. Yesenin stands alongside Blok and Tsvetaeva in the pantheon of Russia's greatest lyric poets and, similar to them, has remained among the most untranslatable. Anton Yakovlev's conscientious handling of the elements of the craft, manage to convey a palpable voice and persona for Yesenin, and persuade us he truly was a major poet."
—Alexander Cigale, translator of *Russian Absurd: Selected Writings of Daniil Kharms*

A Change in the Weather
poems by Ron Kolm

"Open these pages and join Ron Kolm, arch-denizen of New York City, as he picks his way through the lethal and potentially surreal. In Kolm's world, dada is a verb and anything is possible in the mope-eyed bookstores and dystopic subway darknesses he traverses. Expect the unexpected. Charles Bukowski throws shade on Velvet Underground."

—George Wallace, author of *Poppin Johnny* and *Who's Handling Your Aubergines*

King of the Fireflies
poems by Rebecca Weiner Tompkins

"The poet reaches inside herself and waddayaknow! all Nature is there, Worlds within Worlds. And Word by Word she unspools her singular vision, a trail we follow to a shared place. It's lit by fireflies. It's red with life. It's Rebecca Weiner Tompkins at the peak of her powers and she is singing just for you."

—Bob Holman, poet (*The United States of Poetry*) and proprietor of Bowery Poetry Club

Border Crossings
poems by Thaddeus Rutkowski

"There is an eerie and edgy appeal to Rutkowski's spare poems and in his sly, deadpan humor as he takes potshots at an absurdist world. Sometimes playful, ultimately serious, the poet brings an unusual heritage—Polish and Chinese—to his observations. One ends up cheering this poet's curiosity and humanity, wanting more stories, more poems."

—Colette Inez, author of *The Luba Poems*

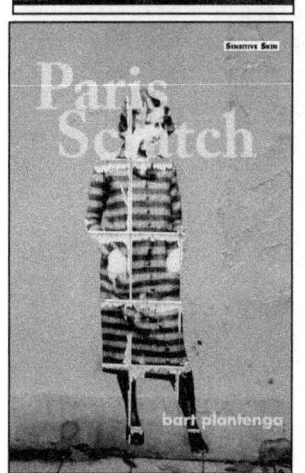

Paris Scratch
snapshots of everyday Paris life, by bart plantenga

"A marvelous book – imagine Baudelaire taking a camera and throwing out his pens and precious inks in a rebellious anti-anti-Dadaist manner, then taking snapshots of everything that comes his way…the author's camera moves very fast, the 'center cannot hold' and we live only twice!"

—Nina Zivancevic author of *Death of NYC*

NY Sin Phoney in Face Flat Minor
snapshots of everyday New York life, by bart plantenga

"Look carefully at these written snapshots to see what lurks below the surface & don't be surprised if you feel a bit self-conscious, frightened, even nauseous at times."

—steve dalachinsky, PEN Award author of *The Final Nite & Other Poems*

Music: Drawing Down the Muse
drawings by David West

"West's talent is of visual emotional representation; from eye to hand to heart. Through these works on paper, ink, guache and color pencil, we become mesmerized by the focused immersion into sound."

—Karen Finley, *Shock Treatment, A Different Kind of Intimacy*

Barefoot in the Heart: Remembering Neem Karoli Baba
an oral history, edited by Keshav Das

"Barefoot in the Heart is a divine raft to take us across the ocean of darkness to the glorious land of light. Every page is filled with Maharajji's nectar.... Profound gratitude to Keshav Das and his collaborators...."

—Jai Uttal

Dime Bag
stories 1978–1986 by Vincent Zangrillo

"If the streets of New York could talk, they would want Vincent Zangrillo to be their voice. The smell of the match under the spoon, the voices shouting two apartments down, a sigh lost in the rush of 10 million people hustling to get through their day, these are the things Zangrillo knows, cherishes and tells. We are blessed to have his unblighted vision of the damned."

—Tom Graves, author of *Pullers and Crossroads: The Life and Afterlife of Bluesman Robert Johnson.*

Why Sing?
poems by John J. Trause

"The range and playfulness of *Why Sing?* answers that question in a variety of lyrical modes. Trause is a one-man orchestra. Anyone who knows who Felix Paul Greve is and quotes him in German is an imp who knows much and isn't shy about taking his singing babes into the agora."

—Andrei Codrescu, author of *The Art of Forgetting*

Backwards the Drowned Go Dreaming
a novel by Carl Watson

"[Watson] writes like someone who pushed himself to the wall, then pushed through it to the void and came back with stories to tell. Here he reclaims the seventies, one of the more desolate of recent epochs, with the clarity of Proust, the balefulness of Bodenheim, and the raw honesty of an Iggy song."

—John Strausbaugh, author of *Black Like You* and *Sissy Nation*

East of Bowery
stories by Drew Hubner / photographs by Ted Barron

"Drew Hubner's prose and Ted Barron's photos are kin, at once raw and lyrical, grit and grace, which is what the city was like back then. The combination is magic, the essence of the time and place."

—Luc Sante, author of *Low Life* and *Kill All Your Darlings*

For more information about these and other books, go to:

www.sensitiveskinmagazine.com/sensitive-skin-books

CPSIA information can be obtained
at www.ICGtesting.com
Printed in the USA
FSHW021814141019
63001FS